BRING DOWN
THE SUN

HISTORICAL NOVELS BY JUDITH TARR

Lord of the Two Lands
Throne of Isis
The Eagle's Daughter
Pillar of Fire
King and Goddess
Queen of Swords

OTHER NOVELS BY JUDITH TARR

The Hound and the Falcon
Queen of the Amazons
Bring Down the Sun
White Mare's Daughter
The Shepherd Kings
Lady of Horses
Daughter of Lir
Tides of Darkness
Avaryan Resplendent
Avaryan Rising

BRING DOWN
THE SUN

Judith Tarr

TOR®

A TOM DOHERTY ASSOCIATES BOOK
New York

BRING DOWN THE SUN

A Tor Book
Published by Tom Doherty Associates, LLC
175 Fifth Avenue
New York, NY 10010

www.tor.com

Tor® is a registered trademark of Tom Doherty Associates, LLC.

Library of Congress Cataloging-in-Publication Data

Tarr, Judith.
    Bring down the sun / Judith Tarr.—1st ed.
        p. cm.
    "A Tom Doherty Associates book."
    ISBN-13: 978-0-7653-0397-4
    ISBN-10: 0-7653-0397-3
    1. Olympias, Queon, consort of Philip II, King of Macedonia, d. 316 B.C.—Fiction.
2. Alexander, the Great, 356–323 B.C.—Fiction. 3. Macedonia—History—To
168 B.C.—Fiction. 4. Greece—History—Macedonian Expansion, 359–323 B.C.—
Fiction. I. Title.
    PS3570.A655B75 2008
    813'.54—dc22

                                                            2008005262

First Edition: June 2008

Printed in the United States of America

0 9 8 7 6 5 4 3 2 1

To all my loyal readers
with thanks

PART I

Polyxena

One

Every morning, even so early in spring, the young men ran in a mob out of the king's house to the practice field. There was still snow in the hollows; the mountains above them were white from crown to foot. But as the sun came up, it warmed, and they stripped off their chitons and ran and fought and danced naked on the new grass.

One particular morning, the late king's daughter watched from the hillside, hidden in the shadows of the sacred grove. She should have been down in the temple, sweeping the floor and tending the lamps like a proper acolyte, and so she would be before anyone happened to catch her. These few moments were hers, stolen from the day and its duties.

The air was almost as warm as summer. It would not last: her bones could feel the cold at the back of it, the final blast of winter waiting to roll off the mountains. Still, today was blessed with beauty, like the men playing at war on the field below her.

The unaccustomed warmth made them lazy. Their dance was slower than usual, their blades clashing almost softly, without their usual ringing clangor. Sweat ran down the long muscled backs and flew like sparks from the curls of hair and beards.

Polyxena leaned forward slightly. Her breath came quick; she was warm inside, melting from her breastbone to her knees. Her hand pressed against rough bark, but in her heart she stroked smooth living flesh. She could feel the blood pulsing in it, and the muscles rolling under the skin. Her tongue curled as if it could taste the salt of sweat; her nostrils twitched at the imagined musk.

She thrust herself away from the tree. Something in the air was making her thoughts all strange. Instead of simple pleasure and appreciation of art well performed, she could only think of what a man's body was best suited for.

It must be that it was spring. The mares were all in season, and the heifers were lowing for the bull. She wanted a bull of her own, a man as strong as she: a hero, a king, a god.

There was no such creature here. As lovely as these young men were, they were merely mortal. She wanted more.

She turned her back on the field. The clash of bronze on bronze went on behind her. Her fingers twitched of their own accord, remembering the weight of a sword.

Deliberately she stilled them. Swiftly, almost running, she descended the hill to the temple that stood in the grove's heart.

Nikandra watched her brother's daughter as she swept the sanctuary. Polyxena seemed unaware of the scrutiny: her head was bowed, her face hidden behind a curtain of red-gold hair. Her movements were brisk, not quite angry; her back was a fraction more upright than it strictly needed to be.

She had been as cross-grained as a she-bear in the spring since well before winter's snows retreated to the mountains.

Last spring she had been very much a child still, with a child's frets and rebellions. This was different: she had grown into a woman, and the powers that woke in her were strong, as befit a daughter of queens.

Too strong, Nikandra thought. If the girl discovered what she truly was, or more perilously, if others discovered it . . .

She, and they, would not. Nikandra had labored long and hard to make sure of it. And so she would do again, as she had done so often before—for the girl's own good, and for everyone else's, too. She wrapped shadows about her and withdrew from the shrine.

Polyxena dawdled as long as she could over her sweeping. She had known all too well that Nikandra was there, watching her. When that keen scrutiny withdrew, she was only slightly reassured.

Her aunt was plotting something. There was a little too much tension in her, and rather too sharp a sense of decisions made and plans set in motion.

That had been true ever since Polyxena could remember. It was a little stronger now, the strangeness a little clearer—as if everyone else knew a secret, but no one would share it with her. Often she felt eyes on her, as if someone or something watched her from afar, and waited, and bided its time; but it was never more than a feeling.

It could drive her mad if she let it. Anger she would allow herself, but madness, no. She was never as weak as that.

She pondered the wisdom of slipping away and hiding in the grove until her aunt's thoughts turned elsewhere, but she had not been born or raised a coward. The floor gleamed as brightly as grey stone could.

Pilgrims were already straggling into the shrine, waiting with varying degrees of patience for the day's priestess to come out of the house she shared with her sisters. There were no great embassies today, no wealthy man or woman with chattering retinue, and no prince or archon in silks and gold. Mostly these were simple people, come to ask the god of the grove or—more rarely now—the Mother to give them good fortune and sage advice.

It was not Nikandra's day to interpret the omens, or she would have stayed in the temple and Polyxena would have had a day's reprieve. She paused to greet the eldest of the temple's snakes, which had come out of its basket to greet the sun. Its tongue flicked her hand, dry and soft; its scales were as smooth as beading under her finger. She bowed and murmured a reverence, then made her way out into the clear morning air.

Just past the threshold she met the eldest priestess, whose name and title was Promeneia. Polyxena bowed as she had to the snake. The old woman stared through her, lost already in the half-trance of her office.

Someday, if Nikandra had her way, Polyxena would walk that same path and perform those same duties. The prospect did not strike her with horror, but in her heart she knew she was meant for other things.

Nikandra was in the priestesses' house with the second eldest of the three priestesses, dark Timarete. They stood at the tall upright loom, weaving the tapestry that had been taking shape since Polyxena was old enough to remember. Every time she saw it, it was a little different: larger or smaller, simpler or more ornate, full of fire and shadow or bright with sunlight and greenery.

Today a skein of fire ran through the new green of spring. It began in darkness and bloomed into the brilliance of a sun.

Polyxena's breath caught. For a moment she was dizzy, reeling as if cast into empty air. Then the earth was solid under her again, and the weaving was simple colored threads on the wooden frame of the loom.

She sat, or rather sank down on weakened knees, on the stool by the door. Timarete smiled in the way she had, as if she knew everything there was to know about everyone she saw—and good or ill, none of it troubled her serenity. She ran the shuttle through to the edge and lodged it there, nodded to Nikandra, and left the two of them together.

Polyxena waited for the blow to fall, for there must be one. Nikandra was clearly in no hurry to strike. She studied her brother's daughter for some time, with no expression that Polyxena could read.

At last she said, "Fetch your veil and come with me."

Polyxena's head was full of questions, but she knew better than to speak any of them aloud. She found when she stood that her knees would hold her up; her steps were steady as she retreated not only to find her veil but, on consideration, to put on a less threadbare gown. When she emerged from her tiny box of a room, Nikandra arched a brow at the transformation but offered no objection.

She led Polyxena out of the priestesses' house and past the temple and the sacred oak. It was the same path Polyxena had taken just this morning, where the grove thinned into the field that lapped the feet of the city wall.

The young men were gone now, back into the king's house. The gate was open as it was every day, with a broadening stream of pilgrims making their way to the oracle. Already

Polyxena heard the ringing of bronze as the oracle woke and began to speak; she almost fancied that she could make out words in that eerie, metallic singing.

She made herself stop straining to hear. It only gave her a headache, and made her stumble as she tried to walk.

None of the pilgrims appeared to recognize Nikandra or her acolyte. Nikandra paid no heed to them, an example Polyxena judged wise to follow. She shivered as they passed under the shadow of the gate, surprising herself with that rush of sudden cold; then she was out in the sun again. The sky was bright and clear overhead, though walls rose around her.

The streets were full of people. It was a market day, and pilgrims as well as townsfolk crowded the square. The Greek habit of keeping women locked in their houses had yet to find its way into Molossia; even women of rank flocked to the market, mingling and chattering and basking in the rising warmth.

Nikandra passed through them without pausing. Polyxena's curiosity had risen, but so had her stubbornness. She would not ask; Nikandra would have to speak.

It seemed they were going to the king's house. That raised Polyxena's brows. They could have gone another way, around about to a much less populated gate, which meant that this must be a lesson. Polyxena was meant to learn something from it.

She knew better than to ask Nikandra what it was. Her aunt would only tell her to think for herself.

The men in the palace and the women in the temple crossed paths less often than Polyxena would like. The king came to the temple when duty or ritual commanded. The priestesses had no such obligations in the king's house, although they could be invited there to give counsel, attend a feast, or—and this Polyxena liked best—to attend the queen.

They were never summoned. That would be lacking in respect. They could choose to go, or they might refuse, which they did far too often for Polyxena's taste.

Polyxena had been born in the temple. If she had been male, she would have been taken directly to the palace and raised as befit a king's son. Because she was a younger daughter of the ancient line, the priestesses had laid claim to her.

Her elder sister Troas had been given to their uncle the king when she was old enough to marry. Their younger brother was still barely old enough to live among the men, but when he was a man, gods and his uncle and the royal council willing, he would be king. Polyxena was the odd one, the gift to the Mother whose grove had stood since long before human memory.

No one had asked her whether she wanted the life that had been chosen for her. She had a calling to the Mother; of that she had no doubt. But she was not called to be one of the oracles here in Dodona. That too she knew in her heart.

Her aunt would not hear these thoughts: she called them childish fancies. Polyxena had learned long since to keep them to herself. If she pressed too hard, she was kept at home when a message came from the king's house; and that, she could not bear. She loved that other world, with its strange horizons and myriad temptations.

It was a world of stone and bronze, hardened leather and hammered gold. The huge dogs of Molossia padded through the corridors and sprawled on the floors. Their masters were of much the same kind: big, tawny-skinned, and irresistibly lazy.

There were no women in the public halls. They kept to their own house and their own counsels. All the visible power here belonged to men.

That was the world's way, but the truth was not so simple. If Polyxena turned her mind to it, she could feel the thread that ran beneath, the subtle force that was the queen. Sometimes it was almost too subtle to find, but it was always there.

Nikandra in her black robe and bare feet walked through these halls like a shadow out of an older world. Those she met bowed—not always with good grace—and murmured words of respect. Whether that respect was real mattered less than that they acknowledged the need for it.

Polyxena attracted a different kind of attention, one that made her raise her chin and straighten her back. She had beauty: her mirror showed it, and so did people's faces. Her aunt never mentioned it, probably for her own good, but Polyxena was blessed or cursed with clear sight.

She knew better than to stare baldly at the men who stared at her. She drew up her veil until it half hid her face. That made them work harder to see the beauty that was there.

Nikandra troubled with no such artifice. She was blessed with height that Polyxena did not have, and she was still beautiful though she was past thirty: a beauty of broad clear brow and long straight profile and waving gold-red hair. She walked as straight as a man, with her head uncovered and her face bare to the world. Few men could meet those cold blue eyes.

Those same men suffered no such compunction when it came to Polyxena. She was enjoying herself much too much; she nearly let down her guard and smiled at a strong young thing who gaped unabashed as she passed. He must be new: she had not seen his face before.

Almost too late she flicked her eyes away and fixed them on
the upright, black-clad back in front of her. When they reached
the passage that turned toward the queen's house, Nikandra
walked on past, somewhat to Polyxena's surprise. She was aiming toward the king's rooms.

Polyxena had never been this far into the palace. She knew
the queen's house well and the great hall well enough, but had
glimpsed the rooms beyond it rarely and never so close.

They were not as open or airy as the queen's rooms, nor
were they as well kept. They were clean enough, but there was
a certain air of dishevelment about them, a careless clutter of
weapons, clothing, and oddments cast wherever their owners
had let them fall. Those owners must be out and about: Polyxena saw only a servant or two struggling against the tide of
disorder, and once a woman barely covered with a bit of
gauze, who squeaked and fled at the sight of them.

Nikandra took no notice of her or, as far as Polyxena could
see, of anything else. She threaded the maze of corridors as if
she knew them well, emerging at last into a place that startled
Polyxena with familiarity: the lesser hall where the king's
Companions spent such idle hours as they had.

Polyxena had been there once before, following Nikandra
to a gathering in the greater hall, but for that she had come in
through the outer regions of the palace. This much more cir-
cuitous path was part of the lesson, then. It seemed Polyxena
was to remark and remember, and take thought for the ways
people lived outside the temple.

Or else she was to reflect that men were untidy, barely do-
mesticated, and sorely in need of setting to rights. That would
be a familiar lesson.

The Companions' hall was in much less disarray than the

rooms behind it. Here the weapons on display were kept bright and polished, and the floor was as clean as it could be when there were dogs underfoot. Only a handful of men stood or sat or lounged on couches: half a dozen in all, and one was the king.

Polyxena spared her uncle a glance, but the others caught more of her attention. They bore a striking resemblance to one another: tall men, light and lean like gazehounds, with hair so fair it was nearly white. Arybbas beside them seemed as darkly massive as one of the Mother's oaks, though in any other company he was a tall and rangy man with hair more red than brown.

He greeted Nikandra with due respect, but the others offered her the full obeisance, kneeling and bowing their heads as if she had been the Mother herself. That was a rarity in these days. Polyxena saw how Arybbas' lips tightened at it, but Nikandra smiled and laid her hand on the eldest man's head. "May the Mother bless and keep you," she said.

The strangers bowed even lower at that. Nikandra raised the eldest, who was old enough to have fathered the rest; they followed suit, as carefully in unison as dancers in a temple. Once they were upright, they all kept their eyes fixed on their feet, even the youngest, who might have been expected to show a glimmer of curiosity.

"Your manners do you credit," Nikandra said. "Be at ease now; it's not the year-king we want you for."

Most of them stiffened at that, but the youngest looked up quickly. His eyes were clear deep blue, and they sparkled with mirth before he lowered them again.

"These are Hymeneia's children," Nikandra said, "from the vale of Acheron. She was never blessed with daughters, but the Mother sent her loyal and obedient sons."

Polyxena wondered about the youngest, but the rest seemed as demure as a maiden was supposed to be. They were lovely boys, soft in their movements, well-spoken and gentle. If they had been a litter of puppies, Polyxena would have been pleased.

She eyed them in growing suspicion. That suspicion bloomed into certainty when her uncle said, "Chins up, lads. Let her take the measure of you."

When they raised their heads, every eye fixed on Polyxena. They were lovely, every one. And not one was her measure of a man.

Nikandra's satisfaction was so strong it lay on Polyxena's tongue like a taste of unmixed wine. She must have scoured the wilds of Epiros to find a clan that still followed the ways of the Mother.

She had done well, by her lights. She had found the last six men in this part of the world who were fit to make a marriage with a daughter of the grove. It was a pity they were not fit to marry a daughter of Achilles.

Two

"I want to marry," Polyxena said. "I dream of marrying. But if I'm given to choose, why must I choose *those?*"

Her sister Troas paused in stitching a state robe for the king. She was a softer spirit than Polyxena, and some said more beautiful: a beauty of milk-white skin and soft hands and wide blue eyes. Still, she was queen, and she had her own share of wisdom.

Her long fingers traced the curve of the embroidery along the hem: gold thread on crimson. One of her maids hastened to fetch a new coil of thread; green, this one, like new grass.

When the needle was ready, she set a row of tiny, perfect stitches. Then she said, "You only have to choose one."

Polyxena tossed her head impatiently. "What's to choose between them? They're a flock of blue-eyed sheep."

"They're handsome sheep," said Troas. "Choose the handsomest and be glad you weren't born elsewhere in the world. Royal daughters aren't given to choose their marriages there, nor are royal sons, either, unless they're very lucky."

"Kings can do as they please," Polyxena said. "I want a king to choose me."

"Any king? Even if he's old and ugly and smells like a he-goat?"

"There are young kings and strong kings. If my king hasn't mastered the art of the bath, I'll teach him."

"You are young," said Troas, who was a whole five years older. "These Hymenides already know how to bathe, and they're young and pleasing to look at, and they'll do your bidding. With them you'll be free to do as you please."

"I want a man," Polyxena said stubbornly, "and I want one who is worthy of me. I want a king."

There was no budging the girl. She had always been headstrong, but with time and training she had learned to rein herself in. She had performed her duties and assisted in the rites of the temple as an acolyte should, albeit with a certain lack of passion.

Now that Polyxena's body was waking to itself, Nikandra had dared to hope for an end to her long vigilance. A young woman distracted by a handsome husband would be safe; once the children came, she would focus her powers on them and not, please the Mother, on more perilous things.

The Hymenides had been the answer to Nikandra's prayer. They were men of the old world, impossibly rare in this graceless age. Nikandra would have thought Polyxena would be delighted to choose a man who had been raised to do a woman's bidding.

But Polyxena was cursed with a contrary spirit. Troas was useless; her attempts at dissuasion only deepened Polyxena's defiance.

Nikandra had her own substantial share of stubbornness. She extricated Polyxena from the queen's house and brought her back to the temple with not a word spoken. Polyxena was obstinately silent, and Nikandra saw no profit in argument.

In the morning, as the first light of dawn struggled to brighten a sky gone dark and cold, Polyxena emerged from her cell and nearly fell over the youngest Hymenid. He sat cross-legged in front of her door, wrapped in a bearskin, rocking and singing softly to himself. The rhythm of his song had crept into Polyxena's dream; her heart was still beating to it.

"Go away," she said.

He rose with grace he must have studied since he was old enough to walk. Her belly tightened in spite of itself. He was not the man she wanted, but he was a beautiful creature.

His voice was as lovely as the rest of him, light and melodious like a trained singer's. "Lady, I can't. I've been commanded."

"I command you to let me be."

"The Lady said you would say that," he said. "I'm to assist you with your duties, and you are to allow it. That's her command, lady."

Polyxena drew a long breath. She should not shriek and rail at this boy; it was hardly his fault that he had been inflicted on her. If anyone deserved a grand fit of temper, it was her aunt.

Nikandra would be expecting it. Polyxena refused to gratify her. With careful calm she said, "Do as you please. Goddess knows it's dull enough."

"Surely not if you're with me, lady," he said.

She ignored his flattery. There was water to fetch and the floor to sweep and the lamps to tend—all in biting cold that held no memory of the previous day's warmth. Only then could they break their fast with fresh bread and olives cured in salt and a cup of heavily watered wine.

He uttered no word of complaint. Even when the sleet turned to snow while they fetched water from the spring that ran only in the daylight and went dry as the sun set, he never failed of his carefully trained courtesy. He shielded her from the wind and insisted that she put on his bearskin, though her woolen mantle was warm enough.

He was an excellent servant. She would have kept him for that.

Only a handful of pilgrims had braved the storm to beg for oracles. Timarete had the unenviable task of sitting under the sacred oak, sheltered from the snow by its branches and warmed by a brazier, and making sense of the song the wind sang as it smote the flasks and jars of bronze that hung from the branches. To Polyxena when she passed, the god's voice sounded like a long and rambling complaint.

It set a thought in her head, which she left to take root and grow. When the temple was in order and the priestesses' comfort attended to, Polyxena had lessons to recite and a heap of mending to do.

Her shadow lent a hand with that; for a man he was deft with a needle. Then she learned that his name was Attalos and that he had been born in the year before her, as near as he could tell. She also discovered that he could sing; his voice was as tuneful as she might have expected.

She did enjoy his company. When she looked at him, the stirring she felt when she watched the king's Companions in the field was barely there. He was too smoothly pretty, and she did not incline toward women or unfledged boys.

Her dreams that night were dark and strange. She danced by moonlight in the sacred grove. The clashing of cymbals and the pounding of feet on the winter-hardened ground echoed and reechoed down the long corridors of trees. Cold light cast darts through the black branches. The night was full of eyes, of shadowy shapes and whispering voices.

In the dream the temple was either gone or not yet built, but the Mother's tree stood tall under the moon. Its leaves rubbed together like hands; a voice spoke from its heart, deep and slow, in a language older than any mortal thing. She almost understood the words; almost comprehended their meaning.

Her body was full of the dance. She had begun in her acolyte's tunic, but after a while it vanished. She danced naked with her long hair loose, whipping her flanks, and the blood-warm air caressing her skin.

The moon and the darkness spoke of winter, but the heavy heat was unmistakably summer. It rose from inside her, like the music and the dance, throbbing in her veins.

A great shape loomed out of the dark: the Bull of Minos with his heavy shoulders and massive horned head, dancing on a man's feet, with a man's body, and a man's phallus but great as a bull's, rampantly erect. For all his size, he was quick, and he moved with ponderous grace.

He was closer to Polyxena's dream of a man than any she had met in the waking world. His dance woke depths in her body that she had never known were there. He was dancing for her: the blunt-muzzled head turned toward her; the dark eyes fixed on her.

Even if she could have resisted him, she would not have wished to. She stepped out into the circle, where moonlight and darkness crossed one another like blades. The music quickened. The hands that gripped hers were breathtakingly strong, but she was no weaker than they—unless she chose to be.

This was the choice she wanted. This was a taste of the power she longed for. Raw as it was, it begged her to master it; to make it complete.

He seized her in the midst of the dance. She was already reaching for him. When his arms tightened, her own were locked around his middle. As he thrust, she opened to him.

Pain was pleasure. Pleasure was exquisite pain. He filled her until she was like to burst—but however huge he was, she was vast enough to contain him. She was the Mother in the living flesh. All that he was, was inextricably a part of her.

She lay in the dark, listening to the wind that wailed through the branches of the grove. Her little box of a room was icy cold, but she was awash in warmth. When she flung off the blankets, the chill hardly touched her bare skin.

Her breasts were taut. When her fingers brushed her nipples, she gasped; a shock of pleasure ran through her. Her hand ran down the curve of her belly to the heat below.

The memory of him was still inside her, a fullness so complete that there was no room for any lesser presence. The milk-and-water boy who slept outside her door was hardly a flicker in her awareness, even as she stepped over him. He murmured words she did not care to catch, and curled up tighter, like a puppy in a litter.

She was naked and barefoot, her only garment her hair, but the fire of the dream was with her even yet. She stepped out into the windy dark, to find that the storm had blown away and the stars were brilliant overhead.

The grove was full of voices—though not those of her dream. Those had come from outside, from watchers who had haunted her dreams for as long as she could remember, although they had never shown themselves in the waking world. These voices were born in the grove.

She had only begun to learn the language of the oracle, but on this night the Mother was in her, with all knowledge of past and present and to come. She stood beneath the Mother's tree in the clangor of bronze and the crying of wind.

Out of sound came light, and out of light came understanding. Her body followed it, dancing to the ancient rhythm.

She bowed to the skill of the priestesses who could transform this glory into words. She had not advanced so far. She could see and feel and understand, but that understanding ran too deep to express.

It was like the tapestry she had glimpsed on the priestesses' loom: darkness shot with sudden fire. The Bull of Minos was in it, and the Mother's snakes coiling together, and the old dance of body and body that gave birth to the sun in splendor.

She stamped and spun, dipped and swayed. The wind caressed her. The starlight tangled in her hair.

The sun was coming. Already it seared her skin. It swelled in her womb and shouted to be born.

She spread her arms wide and whirled until the stars spun away and the darkness came down, soft and heavy as sleep. And still the wind sang.

Three

Nikandra found her niece at sunrise, sound asleep under the Mother's tree. The wind was bitter still, though it warmed as the sun rose; but Polyxena was as warm as if she had been lying beside a fire.

She stirred at Nikandra's touch, languidly, and smiled in her dream. Nikandra shivered. The Mother's presence was so strong it had a taste, like blood and rain.

She shot a glance at Attalos. He sprang to wrap Polyxena in his own mantle and lift her in his arms. He grunted as he stood: she was not tall, but she was solid enough.

Nikandra hardened her heart. The effort would do him good. "Put her to bed," she said, "then take her place in the temple."

He dipped his head in obedience. Nikandra stayed for a while in the ringing of bronze and the rattle of branches, while he vanished into the temple with his burden.

From the time this child was born, Nikandra had watched and waited and prayed. The omens of her birth and the oracles that had accompanied it promised great things—terrible things, things that would destroy the Mother's rule beyond hope of restoration, and give the world over to men and their gods. Nikandra had done everything she could to turn those omens aside, to raise the girl properly and turn her toward the Mother.

If that meant concealing her from any power that might find and corrupt her, keeping her in ignorance of all that she was, and binding her magic so that she could not use it nor be used by any other, then so be it. Above all, if it meant giving her to a man to live crushed and trammeled as women were forced to live in this world, Nikandra could appreciate the irony—but she would do it. It was for Polyxena's good, and the good of the Mother's people.

But Polyxena was persistent in her refusal to follow the path prescribed for her—and it seemed the Mother was inclined to indulge her.

"It is always perilous to stand against fate," Promeneia said.

Nikandra had not seen or heard her coming. One moment there was no one else beside the tree; then the eldest priestess was there as if she had always been, sitting on the oracle's chair, age-gnarled hands folded in her lap.

"I had thought," Nikandra said carefully, "that you shared our visions for this child."

"I shared your fears," said Promeneia. "It seems the Mother's will is otherwise."

"Why?" Nikandra cried. "Why would She suffer the end of the world She made? What profit for Her in giving it to upstart gods and fools of men? Has She lost Her power? Or merely Her mind?"

"No mortal may understand the mind of the Mother," Promeneia said, "nor should any of us presume to try."

Every part of Nikandra resisted that painful truth. She did not want it to be true. She would not let it.

She was not a child; she had learned through hard lessons that not everything she wished for could or even should come to pass. Nevertheless, this she could not accept. The Mother's power in the world had been fading for time out of mind. Nikandra could not and would not let her own flesh and blood destroy it.

She drew herself erect. "Mortal I may be, but I am sworn to serve the Mother with my whole heart and soul. Whatever I can do to keep Her alive in this world, I will do."

"Surely," said Promeneia, "and so shall we all. But this child is not meant for our order. That, the Mother has made clear."

"What, then? What shall we do with her? We dare not open her eyes to what she is, still less reveal her to a world that will transform her into a weapon against all that the Mother has made. Shall we let her uncle dispose of her as kings do with their chattel in these darkening days?"

Promeneia's calm put Nikandra's agitation to shame. Under her dark and quiet gaze, Nikandra subsided slowly, recovering a little of her wonted equanimity.

Promeneia nodded approval. "Be still and listen. The Mother will tell you what She wants of us all."

It was not a rebuke, nor was it meant to be, but Nikandra felt the sting of it. It struck her in her pride.

She had waged war all her life against the way of the world. This child had been meant to carry on what Nikandra had begun: the only one of her blood who had either the strength or the gifts for it. Such strength and such gifts indeed that they were perilous beyond any Nikandra had known; therefore she had kept them hidden even from the one who possessed them, and buried her in the grove where no spying eyes could find her.

The Mother, it seemed, willed otherwise. "What do we do?" Nikandra asked the last and eldest of her order—and maybe the Mother, too. "What is left for us?"

"Not all change is an ill thing," Timarete said, taking shape in the shadow of the tree. "That one will fly high, but she's no black dove of the grove. She looks to the eagle's way."

"For what?" Nikandra demanded. "To be the eagle's prey?"

"Or to be his mate," said Timarete. "Is that so ill, if it continues to ward her against what else she could be and do? For us there will be another acolyte. That boy with the fair face seems willing, and the grove speaks to him."

"He is male," Nikandra said, meaning to end it there.

But Timarete was no more willing than the rest of the world to do as Nikandra wished. "He is willing. At least let us use him while we can, until the Mother sends someone more to your liking."

Nikandra bit her lip. Again she knew the sharpness of rebuke. She was the youngest of the three. They did not stand on rank, for the most part, but age did teach wisdom—and the others had studied longer and searched deeper into the mysteries than she had yet begun to do.

She was not so very different from Polyxena. What she wanted, she wanted with all her heart. When it failed to come to her, she fought for it, no matter the odds.

It was bitter to think of defeat, of changing the path she had followed since the girl was born.

It would not be defeat. It would be victory of a different kind. The calamities that Nikandra had foreseen would only come to pass if Polyxena woke to the fullness of her powers. Nikandra would do whatever she must in order to prevent it.

Nikandra faced her elders who in the ancient way were her

equals. "We'll use the boy, and we'll use the girl, too. We'll let her fly where the wind takes her—but the wind will blow where we direct it, and we will guard her every stroke."

The others nodded as if Nikandra had seen what was clear to them from the beginning. She swallowed the anger that rose all too quickly; once it passed, she rested in surprising calm. She was not about to surrender—not nearly. But she could change her course if she had no other choice.

After the storm and the dream and the dance, it seemed to Polyxena that the world and the people around her had retreated into a kind of torpor. The boy Attalos stayed on in the temple, serving as acolyte and sharing the duties, but he made no move to claim any part of Polyxena, and no one forced her to claim him. The days ran their round as they had for as long as she could remember, with nothing new or different to distinguish them.

She was suspicious of this quiet. It had the air of a trap waiting to be sprung.

Spring ripened into summer. The rites of the Mother passed one by one. Pilgrims came and went, received their oracles and left their gifts and strengthened the gods with their belief.

Every night Polyxena dreamed. It was not always the same dream, but it had the same taste: like blood and earth and heated bronze, overlaid with a flavor that she could only call watchfulness. The Bull of Minos was in it, and the Lady of Serpents, and the voice of the Mother singing through Her creation. Polyxena would wake with her body loosed in every muscle, and one or more of the temple snakes coiled on or beside her, basking in her warmth.

One morning she came back into her body to find something round and leathery-soft nestled between her breasts. It was a serpent's egg. As she sat up, cradling it in her hands, the eldest snake, the Mother's beloved, kissed her cheek with its forked tongue and slithered away into the shadows.

She wrapped the egg in a scrap of wool and tucked it back into the fold of her tunic. It was a gift from the Mother, a sign of favor. It lightened her heart.

It was a promise, too, though of what, she could not be sure. Something new was about to be born. She had learned as a child in this temple that she had only to wait; the Mother would make all things clear.

Patience was a difficult art. She practiced it as best she could, kept the egg close and performed her duties and took her bits of freedom where she could find them. And every night she dreamed of mysteries.

Four

The egg hatched on the day of midsummer, when the day was at its longest and the night, though sweet, was short. In Dodona's temple the ancient rites were only partly observed. They sang the songs and offered the gifts of fruit and grain and danced the decorous parts of the dance, but the deep mysteries, the great dance and the sacred marriage, they passed by.

Polyxena had always found these observances both beautiful and satisfying. This year, under the influence of her dreams, she understood how hollow they were. They were honest as far as they went, and their devotion to the Mother was heartfelt, but it was only a shell of a rite.

There was more to it by far, more depth and more passion and more mystery. This bloodless ritual, this polite and pleasant celebration, left her deeply frustrated. It was not simply that she knew there was more, or that she wanted it. She needed it. Down in her heart, she lived for it.

The fire of her heart stirred the egg into life. As she lay alone in her bed, not quite so far gone that she would seek out the one man in this place—such as he was—the membrane split and the small blunt nose pushed forth, tasting the air with its tongue.

She cradled it in her palm. It was dark, all glistening black—not at all the gentle spotted creature she had expected. She had not seen its like before.

It coiled in her hand, exploring her fingers with the soft tickle of its tongue. She ran a light finger from its head down its supple body. It arched against the touch.

She smiled. Snakes were cold creatures, narrowly focused on food and intermittent mating, but the Mother loved them. So did Polyxena, for their simplicity. There was nothing complicated about a snake.

The life she needed was both more and less simple than the one she lived here. Still cradling the hatchling, she sought out a basket small enough for it, lined with new wool, and laid the creature gently in it. It stirred—not fretful; snakes did not fret. But it seemed to miss the living warmth of her hands.

She knew she should not relent, but the pouch in which she had carried the egg was more than large enough for the infant snake. It lay quiet there, hanging around her neck next to her heart.

She laid her hand lightly over it. The Mother's blessing was warm inside her. It held a promise that she had not much longer to wait.

That serene resolve carried through a single day and part of a night. As it faded, Polyxena felt a kind of despair.

The sense of emptiness—of hunger—had grown worse. It was not the hatchling's fault: she had fed it from a nest of mice that the priestesses kept for just that purpose. The itch in the back of the skull, as if eyes followed her wherever she went, was so strong that she kept spinning about to catch the spy. But there was never anything to see.

In the spring, when she dreamed, the oracle had taken possession of her. Attalos had told her how her aunt found her, naked and burning hot in the snow. She remembered the dream but not the discovery; she had awakened in her bed, decorously covered, and but for Attalos would have thought the whole of it was a dream.

She had had enough of dreams and studied patience. The oracle did as it pleased—that was doctrine. And yet she had heard the priestesses talking now and then, especially the two elders, of turning the power of that place to their purposes.

It was always a high and noble purpose. They framed the questions carefully and shaped the responses to fit the best needs of those who asked. It might be a city seeking advice on a matter of trade, or a king asking whether he should choose peace or war. The answer they gave was truthful, but they might not divulge the whole truth—or they might make it larger and clearer and stronger. Sometimes they might do both.

Even they did not see what was increasingly clear to Polyxena. The oracle was more than the play of wind in a clutter of dangling pots, that only the priestesses knew how to interpret. For all anyone else knew, the priestesses invented all their oracles, and only pretended to hear the gods' voices in the ring and clatter of bronze.

Polyxena knew in her bones that it was real. Whoever, whatever spoke in that place, it was both a guide and a counselor. And maybe, if one's question was framed exactly, it was a shaper of things to come.

She had no proof of that but the slant of an implication.

She did not know the rite or the incantation that would rouse the power. All she had to guide her was a knot in her belly and a memory of dreams.

She had years of training and close study; and she had the blood of the ancient ones in her. Her foremothers had served the Mother since the dawn of time. She was bred and raised and trained to bend the oracle to her will.

The priestesses would beg strongly to differ, if they knew. She was only an acolyte, and a rebellious one at that. Even Attalos, lowly male though he was, was more suited to the task than she.

All the more reason to make the oracle tell her what she was supposed to do. This was not her place or her fate—but what those were, she needed desperately to know.

Even in desperation she could cling to patience. She waited the rest of the night and the day after, kept her mouth closed and her eyes down and did nothing to attract notice. Such preparations as she could make, she made on the few occasions when she could be alone.

She fasted—someone might have noticed that, but she pretended to eat, slipping the bread and cheese and fruit into her gown and feeding it to the birds and the dogs afterwards, and pouring out the watered wine with a whispered invocation to the Mother. As she worked, she let herself become a prayer; when she attended Timarete in the sanctuary and Nikandra by the Mother's tree, she filled herself with the sacredness of the words and the place.

By evening her belly was a singing emptiness. If she had done it properly she would have fasted for three days, but she could not trust to remain undetected for that long. Then it would all be for nothing.

Polyxena waited an endless time for the sun to wander down the sky. The light lingered, it seemed, forever; the day did not want to let go. She slept a little, restlessly, and fed the snake, offering it a newborn mouse. It stalked and throttled and swallowed the tiny wriggling pink thing with single-minded determination.

When it had coiled in its pouch again, with a lump in its middle and sleep washing over it, Polyxena had no more patience left. There was still a glow of light along the western horizon, but all the priestesses were asleep. Attalos snored softly in his cell across from Polyxena's.

She wrapped herself in a dark mantle: the day had been hot but the night was almost cold. Softly on bare feet she slipped out of the priestesses' house.

The sky was wild with stars. There was no moon, though Polyxena felt it coming like the brush of cold flame across her skin. The wind was all but still.

She passed like a shadow through the grove. The stream was silent, its bed empty as it always was at night. She crossed it, slipping slightly on the still-wet stones.

The Mother's tree whispered to itself. Its bronze adornments made no sound, but the broad-lobed leaves stirred ever so gently.

She had brought a jar of wine and a honeycomb to offer the oracle. She laid the honeycomb on a jut of root and poured out the wine as a libation. The earth drank it thirstily. She fancied she could hear the smacking of lips and the sound of swallowing.

There was nothing remarkable about the wine, but something about the night and the errand made its fumes so strong she reeled. Her body was as warm as it was in her dreams; her limbs were loose. She let fall her mantle and then her chiton.

She had done this before in the cold of winter, under a frost-pale moon. These summer stars were much gentler. Their light caressed her.

The steps of the dance were ingrained in her bones. There was a song, too, a chant, a wild ululation, but a last remnant of caution kept that within, in the safety of silence.

Divinity was in her. It did its best to rule her. But even in ecstatic trance, she kept a remnant of herself.

She turned the dance to her own will—slowly, against powerful temptation to let go, to surrender, to become the gods' plaything. She willed the oracle to wake.

Her feet stamped the earth before it. Her hands clapped the rhythm. The ringing of cymbals echoed it: a wind had risen to shake the vessels along the branches.

Then at last she ventured words. "Tell me," she said in the old language, the language of the Mother. "Show me."

The leaves whispered to one another. Bronze rang on bronze. Faint and high and far, the stars sang.

"Tell me what you see," she said.

The whisper rose to a roar, the ringing to a deafening clamor. The oracle was obedient. It told—everything. Every oracle. Every fate. Every—

Her hand swept through the hanging vessels, throwing their song into confusion. "My oracle," she cried. "*My* fate. Tell me what I am. Where am I supposed to go?"

The tumult of voices stopped abruptly. The silence was so complete that she pressed her hands to her ears in dread that the gods had struck her deaf.

The hatchling stirred in its pouch and began to struggle. She freed it before it harmed itself.

Once her hands surrounded it, it quieted. When it moved again, it was only to raise its head. Its eyes sparked like embers in the starlight. It opened its mouth and hissed.

The sound was strikingly like the rustle of wind in leaves. "Mysteries," it said. "The Mother and the Son. The Mother takes the Bull of Minos to herself and gives birth to the sun."

Polyxena looked into those sparks of eyes. They swayed slightly, back and forth, as if with the wind. "That is not an answer," she said.

"Mysteries," said the hatchling. "Oracles."

That was an answer, of a sort.

"The Mother and the Son," it said. Its body coiled tightly. With no more warning than that, it struck her palm.

There was a brief, burning pain, then a slow and delicious languor. Polyxena had no desire to fling off that tiny, unexpectedly venomous thing. She was not afraid. Even if she died, that was her fate.

Better dead than moldering away in this grove. The hatchling twitched itself free with another but more distant stab of pain, and slithered back into its pouch.

Polyxena's knees gave way. She did not mind. She knelt with her cheek against the rough bark of the oak. Above her head, leaves murmured. They were full of secrets, if she cared to remember them.

She lowered her hands, the one that stung and burned and the one that felt nothing, and pressed them flat to the mould of leaves. The earth breathed beneath. Small blind things crawled and ate and bred. They knew nothing of the sun but that it burned.

And yet they fed the oak that stood so high under heaven. Without them it could not have thrived.

The smallest thing had meaning. The priestesses had taught her that. In order to read oracles, one had to look far down below the surface of things. One had to see and feel and smell and taste, and above all understand.

In order to perceive the full light of the sun, one had to immerse oneself in darkness. The Mother was the earth and all that lived in it, and the sky and the sun and every light of heaven. The Son was—what?

That was the mystery. The world changed. The moon grew old. The Mother never died, but She might choose to withdraw from Her creation—to rest, to amuse Herself, who knew?

Polyxena's awareness spread like roots through the earth and grew like a sapling toward the sky. She reached for the sun, drawing it from the womb of the night. She cast it above the horizon.

Five

When Polyxena touched the sun, its fire leaped through her. It struck like a bolt of the gods.

The earth shook. The oak swayed as if in a gale. The mountains trembled; deep in their hearts, fire called to fire.

Too late Polyxena snatched at the powers she had loosed. The ground beneath her pitched and rocked. Somewhere perilously close, she heard the cracking of stone.

The sun reeled in the sky. Human voices cried out; an ashen rain began to fall. Rivers of mud and fire ran down the mountainsides. The earth yawned, gaping to swallow them all.

Polyxena had no spells or incantations, not even a prayer for this. Her wits barely sufficed to fling her flat while the world went mad around her. She had never expected—she could not have imagined—

"Peace," said a voice so soft, so ordinary, that it struck more powerfully than the braying of trumpets. "Be still."

One last time the earth heaved before it sank back into stillness. On the mountain above, even as the fire died, a steep slope crumbled; a fall of rock roared down into the valley. The air was full of noise and dust and terror.

Yet again Promeneia spoke, clear and steady above the tumult. "It is done. Rest now. Sleep."

In the silence that followed those gentle and impossibly powerful words, not even a bird sang. Polyxena ached in every bone. She would gladly have lain buried in ash and tumbled earth until her mind and self all went away, but her body insisted on rising unsteadily to its knees.

The oak had a slight but distinct tilt. The ground had risen on one side of it, forming a new if shallow hillside. The temple stood intact, but a crack ran slantwise from top to bottom of the wall. The stream beside it was as empty as it was at night; no water bubbled in it.

Polyxena staggered to her feet. All three priestesses stood watching her. The younger two were haggard but hale. Promeneia had aged years.

She leaned heavily on the white and silent Attalos. Her body shook with a palsy, but her eyes were clear and quiet. There was no anger in them.

Nor was there in Nikandra's—and that was surprising. Nikandra spread her hands. "This battle you've won," she said. "Pray the Mother you find it worth the price."

Polyxena was braced for wrath and dire punishment. It dawned on her slowly that she had been punished. The longer she stood upright, the worse the pain was.

She was bruised in every muscle and bone, and in parts of her that she had not known existed. When she tried to think past the moment, her mind felt scraped raw. If she had been turned inside out and beaten, she would have felt no worse.

Somehow she walked, because she was too stubbornly proud to crawl. None of the priestesses offered to support her, nor would Attalos so much as look at her. They had enough to do with carrying Promeneia into the temple.

If Promeneia died, it would be on Polyxena's head. She stumbled toward the priestesses' house, but before she reached the door, her feet carried her away from it. She made her way, hobbling like an old woman, through the grove and around the wall toward the king's house.

It was not that she meant to run away from the temple. She was no use to them there. If she faced the truth, she was worse than useless.

She had only meant to demand an oracle. No one had warned her that the earth would try to break because of it. She had done something—raised something—that was not in any of the lessons she had learned so arduously.

And yet the priestesses must have known she could do such a thing. Their lack of surprise and the air of—not ease, but certainly familiarity, with which Promeneia had dealt with the earth's all-but-breaking spoke of knowledge they had not seen fit to share with Polyxena.

What else did they know that she did not?

No one in the king's house could answer the questions that crowded in her, but she would rather have their ignorance than the secrets the priestesses had kept so conscientiously. She hoped they were sorry for it.

Yes, she was angry. Not quite angry enough to do anything worse than she already had, but the sooner she left the temple, the better for them all.

The palace had escaped destruction. There was ash on the floors, jars of wine and oil broken, and men limping or nursing bruised or broken limbs, but the walls had held. In the queen's house, Troas' ladies swept and scrubbed and made the rooms clean again.

Few of them were hurt. The Mother had protected them.

The queen sat in her accustomed seat with a basket of wool and a spindle. She looked flustered, as if she had just sat down.

She smoothed a stray curl off her forehead and smiled somewhat shakily at Polyxena. "You're well. Good. Go and get clean, then help me spin. No matter how angry the gods are, we still need clothes on our backs."

She was wise. Two of the queen's ladies took Polyxena in hand and carried her off to the bath.

The water that streamed down her body was black with ash and mud. Her hair was clotted with it. Troas' women scrubbed her until her skin stung, then anointed her with sweet oils and dressed her in soft clean wool.

She only stirred when they tried to take the hatchling's pouch away. She snatched at that and glared until they sighed and let her keep it, though she had to hold it in her hands while they washed her breast and shoulders. She did let them string a new, clean cord through its neck, blessing the snake's stillness through all that upheaval. When it was safe around her neck again, it stirred and stretched before it went back to sleep.

While her two attendants plaited her hair with deft fingers, she caught herself sliding into a doze. She blinked hard, willing herself to stay awake. Of all things she dreaded, sleep was among the worst. In sleep she might dream, and in dream she might finish what her folly had begun.

Luckily for what peace of mind she had, she was soon done. Clean at last and fit to keep company with a queen, she walked back slowly to her sister's hall.

She felt most peculiar. The oil was sweet and her gown was soft. She could not remember when last she had been so clean.

This was luxury, and she was born for it. She was not made for raw wool and bare feet. She saw beauty reflected in her sister's eyes, and Troas' wonder and surprise and—just visibly—her envy.

Polyxena had beauty to spare, if the queen of Epiros could see her as a rival. The thought made her smile, though she hid it quickly.

She sat on the stool that had been waiting for her and found another spindle in the basket. It was simple work on the face of it, but it took skill to do well. On that day, she was glad of it.

No one came from the temple to drag Polyxena back to her cage. When night fell, there was a bed for her in the queen's chamber.

Troas asked no questions. She was neither dull-witted nor a fool, and she had always known when to let be. There was ample to do in this world she lived in, though Nikandra might sneer at it.

Nikandra had no use for women who, as she put it, made themselves willing slaves of men. She would never reconcile herself to the way of the world.

Polyxena not only could do that, she would make it serve her. She flinched a little from the thought that followed, that forcing the oracle to do her bidding had had dire consequences. That was as much Nikandra's fault as anyone's, for not warning her that such a thing was possible.

Her dreams that night were quiet, ordinary, without power or terror. She spun wool, wove a war-cloak, heard a sweet singer playing on a lyre.

The end of the dream was as vivid as the waking world. She felt life swelling in her belly, and she saw a shadow at the door. Its shoulders were broad and its step heavy.

Just before she saw the man's face, she sprang awake. That was the Mother's jest: to torment her with foresight, but to snatch it away before she saw anything useful.

Maybe it was a true dream. If it was a mere and mortal fantasy, she would cling to the hope it gave her and pray the gods to make it true.

Six

"The Mother and the Son."

Promeneia spoke the words slowly but distinctly. Her voice startled Nikandra, who had dozed off at the eldest priestess' bedside. She had been dreaming that Promeneia had died; it was not far off the truth.

Promeneia lay as still as she had lain for the past three days and nights, gaunt and shrunken in upon herself. The powers she had raised had drained her dry. It was a wonder she had the strength to speak.

Nikandra was exhausted with prayer and invocations of those same powers which had served and nearly destroyed Promeneia. Timarete had given up the fight; she had fallen asleep across the foot of the bed. There was only Nikandra to hear the words that Promeneia spoke.

The old woman said them again. "The Mother and the Son. That is your answer. Let the child seek it there."

"But," said Nikandra stupidly, "where? There are so many places—there is so much—"

Promeneia did not answer. Nikandra began to wonder if she had imagined the voice and the words. They were as vague as the oracle could be, hovering just past the edge of meaning.

Her mind was fuddled with the aftermath of her niece's eruption of power. She still had not focused enough to understand what all of its consequences would be, though the guilt was clear enough. If she had not shielded the child from the knowledge of what she was, this would not have happened. No matter that her fears had been manifold: of the girl's own immense power, of powers in the world that would seize and wield that power for their own purposes, of wrath and destruction and the toppling of empires. By keeping Polyxena in ignorance, she might well have assured that all those things would come to pass.

She rose swaying. As she looked down in the lamplight, she saw the gleam of eyes beneath the withered lids. A third time Promeneia said, "The Mother and the Son. Her destiny is with them."

Nikandra laid her hand on Promeneia's brow. It was cool; not quite as cold as death, but life was ebbing from it. "I have to sleep," Nikandra said—not an answer exactly; more of an explanation.

Promeneia lay silent, breathing shallowly. Nikandra laid a blessing on her and murmured a scrap of a charm.

Maybe it was useless; maybe not. The powers of earth were listening. They might choose to honor the invocation.

Nikandra had forsworn hedge-magic and the workings of common witches when she swore herself to the temple. There was darkness in that path, and loss of will and discipline—all things she had abjured to follow the Mother's path. She was no wild-eyed witch of Thessaly, all filthy rags and matted hair, flying like a bat against the moon.

But she had the magic. The power was in her, if she chose to acknowledge it.

It was remarkably easy to find that way of thinking again, to remember the words and the rituals, the herbs and the smokes and the bones that rattled as if in mockery of the oracle in the Mother's tree.

None of them had anything to do with a dying priestess or a child with more power than any mortal should have had, and no useful awareness of that power.

Nikandra had meant to protect them all, and Polyxena not least. She should have known that such protection was never a wise thing.

Too late now to undo what she had done. At best she could hope to remedy it, and pray the remedy did not simply make matters worse.

Exhaustion dulled her wits and clouded her judgment. She shook from her head the memory of love charms and petty curses, and invoked the Mother's grace on Promeneia.

The air seemed a little lighter for it. The rattle of breath was the slightest bit steadier. Nikandra did not dare to hope for a miracle—miracles were for men's gods, gaudy things that they were. But her despair was somewhat less than it had been before.

The Mother and the Son. The words followed Nikandra from sleep into waking. They were persistently, preternaturally obscure. It was not that she knew too little; she knew too much. There were half a hundred places and things to which one could attach that meaning, and she could not choose among them.

Nikandra was not one to wallow in remorse for doing what

had to be done. She could force her way past this confusion of the spirit.

Here in Dodona, the Mother ruled with Her consort, whom the men did their best to transform into the king of gods. In other parts of the world, She shared the mysteries with Her son, the first and most beloved of Her creation.

Those rites were wilder than the ones Nikandra celebrated. They struck closer to the body's passions. Nikandra would not say she disapproved of them, but they were not the rite she was born for.

Polyxena had that bent of spirit, the wildness that these gentler observances could not satisfy. There was real danger in this: that in the wine and the singing and the ecstatic dances, not only she might find the way to her power; others would find it as well.

That was the danger. That was the reason Nikandra had hidden her for so long, even from herself. Nikandra had to pray that when Polyxena's body awakened, it buried the magic deeper, until there was nothing left to find.

Nikandra left the priestesses' house in the full light of morning, passing by the pilgrims who had waited in vain while four days while the priestesses tended their eldest sister. They reached out, calling after her. Their hands plucked at her skirts.

They called down prayers on Promeneia, offering blessings and wishing her well. Nikandra would not have paused for beggars, but for blessings she would be less than gracious if she pushed on past. She had to stop, answer their crowding questions and reassure them as best she could.

That was not very well, but they were glad of any crumbs she could spare. It touched her heart to see that they were not simply blind mouths and greedy hands. Who knew? Maybe their prayers would move the Mother to heal Her eldest priestess.

As Nikandra passed through the last of them, she met a handful of women coming out of the town. They were plainly dressed and affecting no estate, but Nikandra knew the queen's face too well to be mistaken.

Nikandra looked on her in newborn respect. Troas recognized it for what it was. Her brow arched.

Nikandra caught herself flushing—a rarity, and not one she was glad of. She covered it with brusqueness. "The girl? She's well?"

"My sister," said Troas, "is well cared for."

Nikandra nodded. "I thank you for that."

"No need," said Troas. "Blood cares for blood."

That was a rebuke, though gently spoken. It stung as it was meant to.

Troas smiled faintly. "I've always been invisible to you, aunt. It seemed to me you only saw her. Now I wonder. What do you see? Are we real to you at all?"

Nikandra's spine had gone stiff. "Is that why you came, lady? To give me the sharp edge of your tongue?"

"I thought I might speak the truth," Troas said. "My sister was never meant for this place. Perhaps I might have been, if you had seen me; but I'm content with the lot that's been cast for me. I've spoken with my husband, and he has a solution to suggest—if you are capable of hearing it."

Truth had a bitter taste. Nikandra had heard that said but had never understood how bitter it could be. She swallowed it along with her pride, though it gagged her, and said, "Tell me."

"The Mother and the Son," said Troas. "When the earth tried to break, those were the words I heard in it. When I repeated them to my husband, he recognized them. 'Those are the Mysteries on Samothrace,' he said. He was initiate there when he was young."

Nikandra stared at her niece. There was the answer. It should have been obvious.

The past days had robbed her of any wits or learning she had had. Or had her mind been deliberately fuddled? Were the omens of Polyxena's birth coming true at last? Were powers gathering that would transform her into the weapon that Nikandra had foreseen?

Who, then? Who would, or could, do such a thing?

As with Promeneia's prophecy, the answers were too many. It could be any one of a hundred rivals of Dodona's priesthood, or even someone whom Nikandra did not yet know: some enemy so well hidden that there was only the whisper of a prophecy to mark him.

Nikandra shook herself hard and made her mind focus on the moment, on the thoughts that were safest to think. "Samothrace," she said. "Of course."

Troas nodded. "The king has agreed to send a ship to the isle with a cargo of offerings and such of our people as wish to go. I've asked to be among them."

"And your sister?"

"Yes," said Troas. "We'll sail as soon as the ship is ready."

Her face was tight; she looked as if she was braced for a fight. Nikandra might have offered one, but she had too much to ponder. All the certainties that had bolstered her mind and spirit had crumbled; there was little left to lean on.

This much she could do. "Guard her well," she said. "Never

let her out of your sight, unless someone you trust is guarding her. Let no one near whom you do not know or trust. Will you promise that?"

Troas studied her with dark and steady eyes—remarkably like Promeneia's, if Nikandra would face the truth. "You have reason to fear for her?"

"I might," said Nikandra.

"Is it anything she knows?"

"No."

Troas nodded slowly, as if something she had long suspected had come clear to her. "Someday soon, she will have to."

"But not yet," said Nikandra.

Troas might have had more to say, but she forbore to say it. She turned instead and made her way back to the palace.

Nikandra stood on the edge of the grove and watched her go. It would be a while before she understood fully all of the emotions that stirred in her.

Regret, yes. Guilt. Resignation, perhaps—though that would be slow to grow.

She had done the best she knew how. If Polyxena could be content to live as a pampered princess, then the rest of it might sink beneath the surface again.

The Mysteries in Samothrace would suit her. They were rites of the deep earth and the wine's ecstasy; they celebrated the body's passion and reduced the mind to wordless desire. They were made for Polyxena.

There was power in these ancient rituals. But could the girl control it? That had always been the danger. The omens had warned against it, and every prognostication Nikandra had ventured gave the same result.

In Samothrace they embraced it. And maybe, Nikandra thought, that would do what all her efforts had failed to do. Maybe, if Polyxena had a careful fraction of what she thought she wanted, it would be enough. She would not go seeking any more of it.

The Mother Herself had guided Polyxena toward this path. Nikandra had to trust in Her.

Seven

The wind was brisk, striking foam from the faces of the waves. King Arybbas' ship danced on them, looking ahead with the bright eyes painted on its prow. The striped sail was as full as a bearing woman's belly; the oars were shipped and the oarsmen sprawled at ease, basking in the sun and spray.

Polyxena knelt as close to the prow as she could get, right above the painted eyes. Cold spray stung her cheeks and stiffened her hair.

Close against her breast, the little snake coiled tightly, hugging her warmth. It had no comprehension of all this strangeness, and no power to understand.

It was remarkably like the queen's maids. They yearned audibly for their familiar place, for earth that stayed mostly still and sky closed in by palace walls. Polyxena could no more understand them than the snake could understand her.

Poor things, all of them, not to know the joy that filled her. It was wonderful—glorious. She closed her eyes and tilted her head back and grinned at the sky.

She was as free as a woman of this world could be. Her

sister sat under the canopy amidships, comforting her maid Merope, who was miserably seasick. The other four clung to anything they could find, in terror of this leaping, surging motion.

Most of the sailors were king's men; when they reached the island they would become guards, ready to defend the queen and her women to the death if need be. They were strong men, well built and good to look at. If the world and its wonders had not been so engrossing, Polyxena would have been content to sit and stare at them.

She had never been outside of Dodona before. After her sister gave her the news, she had been too full of excitement to eat or sleep. The queen's preparations had been breathtakingly brief—only a day and a night—but Polyxena had counted every breath and every hour until the king's house and the grove and the temple were behind her.

She had more than half expected that the priestesses would try to stop her at the last, to bind her forever to a place and a priesthood for which she had no calling. But no one barred her way. No stern face watched her from the temple or the grove, and no voice called her back. Even the sense of being watched was absent, as if whatever it was had elected to let her go.

There had been no farewell from within the temple. Polyxena had not expected one.

She supposed she was in disgrace. She did not care. She turned her back on the grove and the temple and let the brown mule carry her as far away from it as she could go.

As they rode out of the steep valley with its lowering mountains, down to the river and the ship and thence to the sea, Polyxena drank in every sight and sound and smell. From mountain tracks still marked by scars of the wrath she had brought on them to fertile valleys to stony shores and the crash of waves, she committed each step to memory, to bring out later and cherish. Even the ship was a wonder, because it was not Dodona.

Everywhere she went, the Mother was. She had been taught as much, but the truth of it was stronger than she could have imagined. Sometimes she was so dizzy she could hardly stand; other times she had to swallow broad grins or gusts of laughter that her companions might take for hysteria.

Where they were going, her sister's women had assured her, this near-ecstasy was nurtured and encouraged. She pressed them for more, but that was all they knew or would say.

"It's a Mystery," said Deianeira before seasickness silenced her. "When we come back, we'll know, too—but we'll have sworn terrible oaths never to tell."

Secrets, thought Polyxena. She wanted to hug herself. Mysteries. Ecstasies. If she could have put on wings and flown, she would have done it, to be there all the sooner.

The isle of Samothrace rose sheer out of the sea. It was as mysterious as Polyxena could have asked for: a landscape of stark cliffs and wind-whipped greenery, dashed about its feet by wine-dark waves.

They came to harbor late in the long summer day. The walled town climbed the hills above them, humming with people like a meadow with bees. They disembarked shaky-legged on the stony shore and saw their ship drawn up and secured amid a throng of others greater and lesser. Theirs was not the greatest or the most splendid, but it was not the smallest, either. Some of the boats were hardly bigger than a cockleshell.

There were people waiting, a man and a woman in long tunics of plain white wool, with their feet bare and their hair unbound. The offered the queen no obeisance.

She however, with wisdom that Polyxena had learned to admire in her, bowed to them as she would to one of the priestesses at home. They inclined their heads in return and beckoned the newcomers to follow.

That night the travelers from Epiros spent in the city in a hostelry for those who would be sworn into the Mysteries. They had come just in time: tomorrow was the great rite, and every room was full.

The queen was separated from her guards, as men and women lodged apart in this place. Troas lost none of her serenity, even when she was crowded into a barracks of a room with a chattering phalanx of mothers and small children surrounding her. Far down the length of the room, over by the wall, sat a woman decked out with gold enough to fill a temple, attended by a flock of all but naked slaves.

"That's a pirate queen," one of the young mothers said while a fat infant sucked at one ample breast and an equally fat girlchild of some three or four years took her turn at the other. "They say her husband is a eunuch—and she's praying the Great Gods to give her a son."

"She'd do better to pray to the nearest pirate," said her neighbor, grinning.

"I daresay she has—but as far as her husband will know, when the baby comes, its father is a god."

They all nodded at that, down the row of cots and pallets.

Not, thought Polyxena, that any of them looked as if she needed to feign a miracle. Maybe they had come to ask the gods to shut the door on their manifest fertility.

"There's a real king here, too," said a woman farther up the hall. "The King of Macedon has come with his Companions to worship the Great Gods."

"Ah," said her companion. "That's not much better than a pirate. They're all raised in a barn up there."

"It's not so bad now," a third said. "He's been pulling them out of the cow-byres, they say, and turning them into an army. He's even taught them to speak Greek."

"Has he taught them to bathe?" the second woman inquired.

"I was downwind of them," said the first, "and they weren't any worse than anyone else. He's a good-looking man, is Philip."

The second sniffed. "I suppose so, if you like big and brawny. I lean more toward a smooth young thing, myself."

"And that's why your husband is a hairy old goat," said the third.

That won a screech and a leap and a scuffle that ended in scratches and pulled hair and sullen silence. Polyxena was careful not to let them see her smile—or they would have turned on her.

Fortunately she had a pretext for turning away: Troas called her to lend a hand with the evening's tasks, setting up the beds and fetching the ration of bread and oil and sour wine that was all any of them was to dine on. Some of the more toplofty pilgrims objected, but the pirate queen took her share with good humor and ate it without complaint.

The bread was hard and full of grit, and the wine was almost vinegar. Polyxena chose to follow the pirate queen's example. As wretched as it was, it tasted better than it looked—and that maybe was a lesson.

As she sat cross-legged on her pallet and ate her dinner, she filled herself with this crowd of humanity as she had with earth and sea and sky. Women of every rank and station were gathered here, eating as she ate and waiting as she did for the great rite and the Mystery. There were slaves in sackcloth and fisherwomen knotting nets to keep their fingers busy, veiled citizens' wives from Athens passing round a jar of smuggled wine so strong the scent of it had made Polyxena dizzy when she passed by, and brawny warrior women from Sparta who looked as if they had left their armor just outside the door.

Polyxena listened shamelessly to the babble of voices. Some she could barely understand, so thick was their accent; others were not speaking any language she recognized. She had thought she knew how wide the world was from seeing the pilgrims at Dodona, but here they were all piled together, high and low, rich and poor, from the sun-shot cities of the south to the chilly sheepfolds of the north.

They were all here for the same reason. Tomorrow, at the dark of the moon, the Mysteries would begin. None of them professed to know what would happen, although there was speculation enough.

The air crackled with excitement, anticipation, and no little apprehension. This Mystery was twofold, said those who seemed to know the most. The first was simple enough, and one might stop there and present one's respects and go away initiate. But if one truly wished to gain what one sought, one would stay and suffer the second—and that was a deeper, darker, stronger thing.

Polyxena was not here to sing a song and wear a garland and pour a cup of wine on the ground. Whatever she was meant to do, the Mother had brought her here to discover it. She would stay for all of it, no matter what it cost her.

In the morning the priest and priestess in white came to guide them all through the city and out past the walls to the holy place. The excitement of the night before had given way to a spreading silence. Even the children were quiet, clinging big-eyed to the hands of mothers or nurses.

The men had come out from another door and fallen into the column beside them. Polyxena could see only those who were closest. There was nothing remarkable there, though a few had handsome faces. Children walked with them, too: boys and young men, too manly to cling to any-one, though some of their elders walked arm in arm as lovers might.

They passed in procession through streets that had seen a thousand years of their like. Polyxena smelled baking bread, spilled wine, a waft of perfume.

Faces peered over walls and out of doorways. Had any of these people gone to the Mysteries? Or were they like the people in Dodona, too familiar with their miracle to find it interesting?

Her stomach growled. They had been given nothing to eat this morning, and only water to drink.

She had fasted often enough in her training, but the first day was never easy. She swallowed the hunger and dedicated it to the Mother. It still gnawed at her, but the sense of virtue softened the pain a little.

The place of the Mysteries lay just beyond the westward

wall. There the mountain descended in three narrow terraces, each divided from the other by the steep banks of a swift river. It was a wild place despite its closeness to the town, a place of rock and water and swift-scudding cloud, bounded by the mountain and the sea.

As Polyxena crossed the worn stone bridge onto the first terrace, she nearly fell to her knees. For all the crowd of people around her and the weight of the town behind her, she felt as if the Mother's eye had fixed on her and her alone.

She glanced to either side. No one else seemed unduly disturbed. Some were frowning, some smiling; many looked about, wide-eyed with curiosity.

Polyxena shut her eyes and let the current of the crowd carry her onward. The scent of thyme was everywhere, green and strong, and the humming of bees, and far away the roaring of waves. The wind was cool on her cheeks; the warmth of bodies surrounded her, keeping her safe. She was as well warded here as she had ever been in Dodona—and that was a thought she needed to ponder, later, after this was over.

She passed over the river onto the first of the terraces, treading a path that feet had trod for time out of mind. The memory of those older pilgrims was all around her. If she sharpened her senses, she could see and feel and smell them, and hear their voices speaking, echoing down through the years.

They had all come for the Mother, because She had called them or because they had need of Her. Polyxena would have liked to kneel on the Mother's own earth and dig her fingers into it, but the current of people was too strong.

It surged like water onto the first terrace and spread toward and around a hollow paved with hewn stones. In the center stood an altar. Men and women in white waited there, with their heads covered and their faces veiled.

The altar was banked with garlands of flowers and greenery, piled high on the stone table and tumbling over the sides to the pavement. Acolytes in short tunics gathered them up and passed them to the pilgrims.

The one that came to Polyxena was of myrtle, deep green leaves potent with fragrance. She breathed it in. It was sacred to Aphrodite, who was one of the many faces of the Mother.

The priests at the altar raised up a milk-white lamb and a night-black kid. Neither struggled: they rested at ease in the priests' hands. Their blood sprang across the pale stone of the altar and stained with vivid red the last of the garlands.

As the smoke of the sacrifice rose up to heaven, a priestess with a deep pure voice began to chant a hymn to the Mother. It celebrated Her as ruler of the wild places, mountain goddess, Lady of lions. Then it shifted, turning to a wilder mode, to sing the praises of Her son who was also Her lover, god of wine and laughter, brother of panthers.

There was a strong rhythm in the chant, the beating of the heart and the heat of the body as it moved to match the pulse of the ancient words. This rite worshiped Her with dance, and its words and music were meant to stir the blood.

Already among the crowd, people were moving in time with the chant. Polyxena's feet had found the rhythm; her body swayed of its own accord. The scent of the myrtle wrapped her about, drowning the smell of mingled humanity.

As she danced, faces whirled past her, crowned with garlands: male and female, old and young, beautiful and ugly and everywhere between. Dancers came together in circles and skeins, although a few went on dancing alone as Polyxena did.

Troas and her women spun in a circle, linked hand to hand. Polyxena's demure sister had let her hair fall out of its tight braids; it streamed behind her. Polyxena had not known she had such wildness in her.

A line of men danced and stamped beyond the queen and her maids. They were big men, liberally ornamented with scars; their hands looked oddly empty, as if they should be carrying weapons or shields.

Polyxena's eyes found the man in their center, stopped and stayed. He was not the tallest of them, but he was one of the broadest. His hair was thick and black; his beard was cut close. It was vigorous, though not quite as black as his hair: in the fitful sunlight it had a reddish cast.

His face behind the beard was blunt but well-cut, solid and strong. It matched the shape of him, his wide shoulders and muscled thighs. She would not have called him handsome, but he was all of a piece, with a compact, powerful grace.

Now that, she thought, was a man. Her first thought was of a bull, but *lion* fit him better. A young one, a little short of his prime, with his black mane still growing in and his body showing the last faint hint of youngling awkwardness.

He paused in his dance. His eyes lifted to hers. She had expected them to be dark; it was a shock to see that they were blue—as blue as the sky overhead, bright with a fierce intelligence.

They widened as he took in the sight of her. She had heard from the queen's women that a man's regard could make a woman feel beautiful. Under that hot blue stare, she understood how deeply true it was.

She was too wise to smile and too proud to look away. She held her head high under its crown of myrtle and deliberately, slowly, danced for him.

Eight

Even in her dance, Polyxena held to awareness of the world around her. It was a useful skill. Priestesses cultivated it.

She saw how the priests left the altar with the dance still whirling, and how a company of white-robed acolytes moved among the dancers. Those nearest the far side of the circle were led or herded one by one into a low stone temple.

She, near the midpoint of the crowd, had a while to wait, but her feet were light and her body tireless. The Mother was in her, filling her with strength.

The dark man had stopped his own dance to watch her. When the crowd moved, emptying toward the temple, he stayed level with her.

She let the dance slip into stillness, but kept the memory of it as she followed the flow of pilgrims. That was enough to keep his eyes on her. She was careful not to stare at him, though she was aware in her skin of his every move.

So intent was she on the dark man that the door of the Mystery took her by surprise. Troas and her maids had already vanished inside. The narrowing of the stream of pilgrims had shifted the dark man some distance behind her, but she could feel his eyes on her back.

She drew a steadying breath and stepped forward into darkness.

Slowly her sight came back. The space she stood in was old—as old as Dodona, and as holy. The walls around her had not stood so long, but they were built on ancient foundations.

Hands reached out of the dimness. She could just see the bodies beyond, dressed in white. They tugged at her clothes. She willed herself to stand at ease.

They stripped her with deft dispatch, poured gaspingly cold water over her and sealed her brow with blood from a much-stained bowl. While she stood with chattering teeth, the unseen servants covered her with a thin white robe that clung to her damp skin.

Polyxena was glad then that she had yielded to impulse and left the hatchling in the pilgrims' lodging, safe and warm in its pouch. When it was grown it would be a sacred snake, the Mother's beloved, but it was too young and fragile for this.

The hands led her across the ill-lit space. Shapes loomed in it, standing in ranks along the wall. They were carved of stone, squat and overwhelmingly old.

Half of them were female, each with pendulous breasts and pregnant belly and deep slit of the vulva. The rest were male, thick and bandy-legged, flaunting the rampant phallus. They were ugly and crude and irresistibly powerful.

"Here is the Mystery," said a veiled priestess, taking shape beside her.

"Here is the truth," said a priest who had not been there a moment before.

"Female and male, woman and man. The Mother made them both." Their voices mingled, echoing in Polyxena's skull. "One cannot be without the other. They are all one."

The priest slid something cold and strange onto Polyxena's finger. It was a ring, and it made her skin prickle. She stiffened against the urge to fling it off.

It was a thing of power. Once she had accepted that, it was easier to bear.

The priestess knelt and bound a long belt of linen about her waist. Its color was too dark to discern, but in sunlight she thought it might be crimson.

"Ring and girdle will guard you," the priestess said as she rose. "Keep them close and tend them well."

"Now you are initiate," said the priest. "Praise to the Mother and the Son, the Great Gods and the Sacred Brothers."

"Praise be," the priestess said, half-chanting.

While they spoke, they led Polyxena through the temple. Just before they thrust her through the door, she dug in her heels. "I'm not done. There's a second rite, isn't there? I want that—I want more. Tell me how to get it."

"Be careful what you wish for," the priestess said.

And the priest said, "Do you know what you ask?"

"I know what I must do," said Polyxena.

The priestess stood perfectly still. "You would pass the gates of death and face what lies beyond?"

"Whatever it is," Polyxena said steadily, "I am meant for it."

It was impossible to tell behind the veils, but she suspected that her guides exchanged glances. If so, there was no telling what those glances meant.

"Come with us," the priestess said after a pause.

Polyxena's hands were icy, but the chill of fear only made her the more determined. She had come here for the Mysteries. She would stay for all of them.

Her guides turned aside from the door that must lead back to the terrace. Instead they sought one lower, smaller, and darker, that led down by rough-carved steps into the darkness.

The air that wafted up had a cold smell, like damp earth and old graves. Past the first handful of steps there was no light at all. Polyxena could not stop or turn: the priestess ahead and the priest behind kept her moving down into the darkness.

After what seemed a long while, the steps ended. She stood on what felt like packed earth, in a space that might have been as wide as a cavern or as narrow as a grave. When she stretched out her hands, they found only air.

Her guides had vanished. So, when she stepped back, then searched frantically with groping hands, had the stair. She was alone in the dark.

With a strong effort of will she slowed her breathing and quieted her heart's pounding. Maybe she should have explored her prison, but she judged it best to stay where she was and wait. She sank down on the hard earth, drew up her knees and clasped them and rested her forehead on them.

Time stretched until there was nothing left of it at all. The Mystery she had been shown ran through her mind again and again. It was the truth she had been looking for—though in accepting it, she had set herself against everything she had been raised to be.

She had already done that when she left the temple in Dodona. She sighed and closed her eyes—as little difference as that made in this place.

She let memory take her, as vivid as a dream. It gave her bright sunlight and fierce blue eyes and a strong-boned, broad-cheeked face.

Warmth flooded through her; her breath caught. Then darkness did not matter at all, nor was she lonely or afraid. He was with her as surely as if he had been there in the flesh.

She was almost sorry when a hand fell on her shoulder and a voice said, "Rise; follow." Polyxena raised her head and opened her eyes, blinking in blinding light.

It was a lamp, flickering in a woman's hand. The priestess was veiled in white, faceless and all but formless. Polyxena rose stiffly, stumbling until she had her feet under her.

She had no sense of where she was or where she went. The light illuminated nothing beyond the priestess' body. The path on which she guided Polyxena went straight ahead and then sloped sharply upward.

Then at last Polyxena had the sense of walls: they closed in all around her, so that she had to stoop and crouch, then crawl on hands and knees. The taste of earth was in her mouth. Roots brushed her cheeks.

The priestess' light led her onward, but she could no longer see the woman who carried it. The tunnel narrowed until she wriggled on her belly like one of the Mother's snakes.

She began to wonder if she would be trapped here; if the Mystery was slow and suffocating death in the deeps of the earth. She was not afraid of death, though the pain of it might give her pause.

She pressed on as she did everything in this life, with all the strength she had. She clawed through roots and burrowed in earth.

She burst into light: moonlight, firelight, and the low hum of voices chanting. The mountain's shadow rose above her. The sea glimmered below. Robed figures surrounded her.

They all wore the dark belt that bound her own waist; on the finger of each left hand, the dark circle of a ring stood out, distinct in the firelight. Part of her recognized the lower terrace of the Mystery. The rest laid no single name on this place. It was all holy places in one, a long shallow curve of stony ground set apart from the world by the swift torrent of a river.

A figure loomed by the fire. Her heart stopped and then began to beat hard. He was tall, taller than a mortal man, and his horns spread wide beneath the moon.

The Bull of Minos waited for her, that mingled monster with his man's body and his bull's head. His shoulders were massive, gleaming as if with oil; his breast and belly were thick with curling hair. The phallus that rose at the sight of her was as great as a bull's.

She walked through a shower of fragrant petals. The garland of myrtle was still about her brows; its scent rose again around her, as strong as if the garland had been made new again. As she walked, her garments unraveled, falling away from her body.

She made no move to cover herself. Her skin was as hot as if she had stood in the fire. Her hair escaped the last of its knot and slithered down her back.

A shrouded priestess appeared in front of her, rising as if out of the earth. In her hands was a mask. It was old beyond age, carved of alabaster, featureless but for the slash of nose and the long slits of eyes.

It fit to her face as if it had been made of skin and not of stone. The age of it, the power that was in it, froze her briefly where she stood. If she brought down the mountains here, where would she go? What shrine or nation would take her?

The earth held its place. The power that filled her was pleased to stay within the bounds of her body. The Mother's arms embraced her. Whatever strength she had, this place was strong enough to contain it.

The Bull's horned head rose above her. The smell of him was pungent yet pleasant, compounded of sweat and musk and surprising sweetness: honey and thyme, sharpened with smoke.

Her hands ran down his arms. They were massive, but the skin was unexpectedly smooth. The heat of his blood matched hers.

He trembled under her touch. He was afraid: he, the great bull. She smiled behind the mask.

She was dimly aware of the circle in which they stood, the priests and pilgrims beginning a slow chant. The words did not matter. The sound was the spell, the slow rise and fall like the breathing of a great beast.

She had seen this in dreams. The oracle had given it to her, this vision, this truth that shaped everything she would be.

She laid her hands on the Bull's breast. His heart beat hard. So did hers, but she was not afraid. She was dizzy with exaltation.

This was the great rite, *Hieros Gamos,* the sacred union of the Mother and Her chosen. The Bull looked down at her with fierce blue eyes. She laughed aloud and mounted him there, locked her legs around his middle and took him deep inside her.

There was pain, but it was nothing. For every great victory there was a price. That was the world's way.

He bore her weight easily, held her in his strong arms and lowered her to the ground. It was softer than she had expected: grass grew in a circle there. Its sweetness mingled with his heavy musk and the sharp green scent of myrtle.

He wanted to take her as a bull the cow, but she would not suffer that. Face to face and breast to breast, like equals, they worshiped the Mother in all Her glory.

Nine

Polyxena sat enthroned in the Mother's stead, clothed in flowers. Priests and pilgrims brought her offerings of flowers and fruit, sweet cakes and strong wine.

The Bull and his companions danced for her. They put on armor and filled themselves with wine and danced the wild, clashing dance that was sacred to the Great Gods and the Divine Brothers.

It was a vauntingly male thing. Polyxena, raised in a staider observance, was mildly shocked. Yet her body loved the ferocity of it, the leaping and stamping and the clangor of bronze. When they raised their war-cry, she gasped; then she laughed.

It was a splendid noise before the Mother. But they danced it for her—for Polyxena, the living woman behind the Mother's mask.

With the dawn, Polyxena returned to her mortal self. The terrace of the Mystery was strewn with bodies, sleeping tangled in one another or drowned in wine. Even the priests had given themselves up to the rite.

There was wine enough in her, but it made her mind clearer

instead of clouding it. She left the throne, treading lightly on trampled garlands and bruised petals. The morning air was cool on her bare skin. Between her legs she ached, but that was almost pleasurable.

The Bull lay sprawled by the riverbank in a circle of snoring men. In this pale light his head was obviously a mask, though wonderfully wrought. It had fallen askew.

Gently she took off the mask of the Mother and laid it on the grass beside him. Then she worked the Bull's mask from his shoulders.

His hair was flattened and tousled, his cheeks flushed above the curls of his beard. She brushed his lips with a kiss.

His eyes sprang open. His hands caught her before she saw them move.

She made no move to pull away. His scowl lightened. He did not let her go, but he held her somewhat less fiercely.

"You're not afraid of anything, are you?" he said.

"Should I be afraid of you?"

She asked the question honestly. From his expression, he had to be sure of that before he answered. "Cross me and you'll regret it. Challenge me and I'll fight back—and if you blink, I'll win. I don't fight to lose."

"Nor do I," she said.

"We could kill each other," he said as if to himself.

"Or we could fight side by side." She slipped free of his grasp but stayed where she was. "You can't be any less than a king."

"Why? Are you a queen?"

"My sister is," Polyxena said.

He sat up. It was fascinating to see how he changed from the bull in rut to the king in council, eyes narrowed as he considered all the possible sides of her. "Epiros?"

She nodded, then said in response, "Macedon."

It was not a question. He grinned, baring strong teeth. "It seems we're the only proper royals here this year—pirate queens aside. Convenient, don't you think?"

"The Mother disposes us as she wills," Polyxena said. She knew she sounded prim. She refused to be embarrassed by it. "I'm a child of queens. From the very beginning the Mother has loved us."

"They say you're descended from Achilles."

"They do say it," she said.

"And you? What do they call you?"

"Polyxena," she said.

"Odd choice of name," he said. "Didn't she betray your noble ancestor?"

"Some say she did. Others say she did what she could to save Troy. Yet others," said Polyxena, "said he was besotted with her, and demanded her sacrifice on his tomb, to be his consort in Elysium."

"With all respect, lady, I can't see you submitting to any such thing."

"It is unlikely," she said.

He sat up in a strong surge. Polyxena quelled the leap of startlement, so that he only saw how quiet she was, composed and calm. The heat of him made her breathing come shallow.

He lifted the garland from her brows where it had been all night long. It was barely withered; its scent was nearly as strong as ever. "I give you a new name," he said, "a fitting name. Myrtale, crowned one, beloved of Aphrodite."

Polyxena frowned. Part of her resisted; it clung to the old and the familiar. But the sound of the name in his deep burr of a voice, and the meaning of it, fit for a queen, had a rightness that melted her resistance. "Myrtale," she said. "I'll be Myrtale."

He laid the garland aside. Even as he reached for her, she took him as they said a man took a woman, swiftly and by storm.

She left him exhausted, breathing hard and slicked with sweat. Her knees tried to wobble as she walked away, but she held her gait steady.

She picked her way down the steep bank to wash in the stream. The water was snow-cold. The shock of it on heated skin had a peculiar effect: it made her want him all over again.

He was spent. In that much Nikandra had been right: males had no endurance.

She toyed briefly with the thought of finding another man among the fallen and initiating him, too, but the ache inside and the practicality she did not often admit to convinced her otherwise. In the old world, the more men she bound to herself, the greater her power. But in this one, a woman had to tread more carefully.

The man who snored on the bruised grass was a king—a ruler over men. Through him she bound them all.

She scrubbed the blood from her thighs and the sweat from her skin. Sweet herbs grew by the riverside; she perfumed herself with them. There was nothing to clothe herself in but her thick red-gold hair, but she chose not to go searching for a garment among the fallen revelers.

They were waking as the sun came up over the mountain, stirring and groaning and staggering to their feet. She walked among them as if she were still the Mother's image.

Who was to say that she was not? They opened a path for her. Some bowed or murmured snatches of prayer.

A pair of priestesses met her on the first terrace, a few long strides from the city's gate. They dressed her in silence. She was sorry to lose the freedom of the air on her skin, but the mortal world had risen with the sun, and it had its difficulties with the ways of divinity.

She put on mortality with the soft new-woven wool and the demurely plaited hair and the veil. The world muted around her, but she kept the memory of that other self. It would come back to her when she needed it, or when the Mother willed.

Her sister had nothing to say, though her sister's women eyed her sidelong. The pilgrims who had gone no further than the first Mystery were dispersing as the morning brightened, scattering to their ships. Troas might have done the same, but she had waited.

Polyxena, who must learn to think of herself as Myrtale, could not tell what she was thinking. Troas offered no awe, but neither did she seem to disapprove. She simply rose from the bed where she had been sitting, stitching a bit of needlework. "Good. You're back. The men are waiting."

She did not ask if Myrtale had broken her fast. Maybe that was punishment.

Myrtale was not hungry in any case. She had been so full of the Mother that her stomach had forgotten how to be mortal.

The men from Macedon were on the shore, preparing to embark on a ship of somewhat more size but rather less opulence than the ship from Epiros. Their king loaded cargo with the rest of them, wearing no mark of rank and claiming no signs of respect. But Myrtale would always know him.

There was a sort of contract between them, an agreement that needed no words. One glance spoke for both.

I'll send for you, his eyes said.

Her own lowered in assent. *I'll be waiting,* the gesture promised.

Macedon's ship set off first, raising a sail the color of dark wine, with the bright rays of a sun painted on it. Myrtale's heart contracted at the sight. It was not exactly as she remembered from her vision of darkness shot with fire, but near enough.

This the Mother had meant for her. And she was meant to take it with both hands.

But first she had to look on her own mountains again, to come once more to Epiros. For her, everything began there. Even this.

It was hard to climb into her sister's ship and not his; to see him sail away and not know for certain when they would meet again. That they would, she knew surely. But it would be in the Mother's time.

"Soon," she said under her breath as the oars began their steady rhythm, carrying the ship out of the harbor. "Please the Great Gods, let it be soon."

PART II

Myrtale

Ten

The embassy from Macedon clattered into the king's house of
Epiros a month to the day after Myrtale had returned to it
with her new name and her new secrets. They had come over
the mountains on horseback, riding with a bravura that made
the young men of Epiros sit up and take notice.

Myrtale knew better than to expect that Philip would have
come for her himself, but she was a little disappointed even so.
Patience was not her strongest virtue, and she had waited for a
month and had meant to wait longer.

The man who came in Philip's stead was big as all these
Macedonians seemed to be, with a long lantern jaw and a
pleasantly ugly face. His name was Lagos; he came of a noble
house, some said royal—though he said nothing of that. Myrtale gathered it from the servants' gossip.

They gossiped, too, that the king had sent an ugly man on
this errand for cause; he would hardly want his bride to fall in
love with the messenger. But Myrtale reckoned that a false-
hood. Lagos was a capable man; his mind was keen and he
spoke well. Macedon was honoring Epiros with the best it
could spare.

He brought gifts for the king, fine armor and weapons and a team of horses with a gold-inlaid chariot; to the queen he offered a bolt of Persian silk, a silver mirror, and a vial of perfume from Egypt. For Myrtale there was a box of fragrant myrtle wood, and in it a golden diadem.

It was a grand ceremony in the king's hall, with the queen and her ladies in attendance. They all knew what Lagos was going to say; there was no mistaking the purpose of his embassy, once Myrtale had opened the box and taken up the diadem. The murmur that ran through the hall had an edge of excitement.

It was a great thing, this matter of royal marriage. She fought for patience, and for the calm that befit a queen. Troas set the example; Myrtale wondered fleetingly if it had ever been so difficult for her. She was as gifted in serenity as Myrtale was in attacks of fiery temper.

Lagos, thank the Mother, did not waste time in indirection. Having offered gifts and respect, he looked Arybbas in the face and said without further preamble, "My king asks leave to take your niece to wife. He saw her in the Mysteries, and the Great Gods inclined his heart toward her—and toward the alliance that the marriage would offer. This is meant to be, he says. He hopes your majesty will agree."

That was blunt enough. Logical enough, too. But Arybbas was not a hasty man. "We're honored," he said, "that Macedon reckons us worthy of alliance. Still it's my duty to ask: What does he want of her? Wife or concubine? Will he make her queen?"

"My king will take her in lawful marriage," said Lagos, "and give her all honor and respect due her lineage."

"That doesn't answer my question," Arybbas said. "How

many wives does he have now? Four? Six? One has a son, I hear. My niece is a daughter of Achilles and an initiate of the Great Gods. She's more than a trophy to hang on your king's wall."

Myrtale stiffened when her uncle spoke of other wives. She had known she was not the first wedded wife to come to Philip's bed. Everyone knew that kings married early and of-ten. But that was not the same as hearing it spoken.

Lagos seemed unoffended by Arybbas' plain speaking. "My king has wives, yes, as kings do. It's his duty. But he'll honor your kinswoman in all ways, and treat her as the royal lady she is. He loves her, lord king, and worships her as Goddess incarnate."

"That's well and good," said Arybbas, "but love dies. What's left then?"

"This love will last," Lagos said before Myrtale could burst out with it. For that she began to love him—though not as she loved his king. "But even supposing it does not, there's the al-liance of Macedon and Epiros against common enemies, a share in trade and amassing of wealth, and for the lady, the re-spect and position of king's wife."

"But not queen."

Myrtale could not tell if Lagos found her uncle's persis-tence annoying. He seemed possessed of endless patience. "That may be negotiated."

Arybbas nodded. "I'll think on it. While I do, you'll enjoy our hospitality. Whatever you want or need, my servants will see to it."

Myrtale did not see what there was to think on, but she could hardly say so. She was only here on sufferance; if she spoke out of turn, she could be sent away like an obstreperous child.

It was hard to keep the spate of words inside. She was glad to withdraw with her sister, to retreat to the queen's house and gnaw her frustration in peace.

Peace was not exactly what she found. The servant who had presented Philip's gifts followed Myrtale out of the hall, carrying the box with the diadem. At the door to the queen's house, Myrtale tried to take the box and dismiss the servant, but the woman would not go.

"I belong to you now, lady," she said.

Myrtale's brows rose. She had never had a maid. Since she left the temple, she had shared her sister's women, but she had felt no need to claim one of her own.

This was a young woman, smaller than Myrtale—who was not tall herself—dark and slight and quick, with eyes that missed nothing. She wore no mark of slavery; her gown was plain but well woven, and she carried herself with evident pride.

Something about her caught and held Myrtale's attention, though she was ordinary enough as far as beauty went. There was more to her than met the eye.

Eye, thought Myrtale with a shiver down the spine. Those eyes were familiar somehow. As if she had seen or felt them before. As if . . .

"I think," said Myrtale, "that you need an explanation."

Philip's gift grinned. Her teeth were white and strong and somewhat sharp. "What, do I baffle you, lady? My name is Erynna; I come from Thessaly. The king wanted someone fitting to serve his new queen."

"So," Myrtale said, "he does want a queen."

Erynna spread her narrow hands. "Men like to pretend life is complicated. They're such simple beasts, you see."

"You sound like my aunt," Myrtale said.

"Then your aunt is wise," said Erynna. Her eyes darted toward the door, which had long since closed behind the last of the queen's women. "Are we going in, lady?"

"In a moment," said Myrtale. "After you tell me true. Does he want me still? Or am I simply a hook he'll set in Epiros?"

Maybe she had been a fool to ask such a thing of a woman she had barely met. But she trusted her instincts, and those told her this stranger would give her an honest answer— whatever else she might do or be.

Erynna tilted her head slightly. Her lips pursed. She said, "He wants Epiros. He wants everything, that one. He'll take Greece. If he can, he'll stretch his hand to Persia. And," she said, "he wants you. He hasn't touched another woman since he came back from Samothrace. At night he dreams of you. By day he broods, and when he sees a red-haired woman or a boy with long red hair, he roars like a bull. People say you've cast a spell on him."

"There was no need," Myrtale said. She wanted to laugh and clap her hands and dance down the corridor, but she had been studying dignity. She allowed herself a smile and a lightening of her step as she opened the door into the queen's house.

Arybbas took an unconscionably long time to ponder Philip's embassy. Lagos seemed content to wait. There was hunting, there was revelry, there were games on the field where Myrtale had so often watched the young men at play.

She had begun to feel the ways in which her choices had trapped her. As a priestess in the temple she could have escaped to watch the games, but as a princess in the palace she should not sully her eyes with the sight of naked men.

She had no desire to go back to the temple. She did not even know if Promeneia still lived. She refused to ask or to care.

She confined herself to the daily round of a royal lady, spun and wove fine crimson wool into a cloak for her husband to be and listened to the singer who had come up from Corinth to explore these wild outlands. In the mornings there were inspections of kitchens and servants' quarters and the small but airy room where the queen dried herbs and brewed medicines. In the evenings the women dined together apart from the men.

By the fifth day she had had enough. Troas' example of unruffled serenity no longer inspired her. Philip's gifts were a constant reminder of the choices that she wanted to finish making.

Her new maid was deft and impeccably skilled. Myrtale would have wagered that Erynna liked to chatter, but she maintained a decorous silence. *She* had the art of patience.

There was a time to cultivate patience, and a time to declare, *Enough.* Myrtale finished her day's stint at the loom, then put on a fresh gown and instructed Erynna to plait her hair. The little snake had outgrown its bag around her neck; she cradled its basket in her lap while the snake explored her arm and, after a moment, coiled around it.

Erynna was as silent as ever, but her eyes were bright. She moved cautiously around the small and deadly creature.

Myrtale coaxed the snake back into its basket and laid it carefully in the corner where the sun shone most brightly in the day. As she straightened and turned, she found Erynna close behind her.

The girl seemed determined to follow wherever she went. Myrtale opened her mouth to order her away, but closed it with the words unspoken. If she was to be a queen, she had to lose her predilection for solitude. No queen was ever alone.

When Myrtale left the queen's house, Erynna went with her, as silently attentive as ever.

The games were in their third day, but the king had not yet gone out to officiate. Myrtale found him after some searching, in the courtyard by Achilles' shrine where the morning sacrifice was long since over. The day's offerings of fruit and flowers and the bones of a young kid wrapped in fat were wilting or had gone cold, but the king took no notice.

He was deep in conversation with a figure Myrtale had not seen or wanted to see since she walked away from the temple. At first glance Nikandra was the same as ever: tall and robust in her black robe, with her hair uncovered and her feet bare. Then Myrtale saw how thin her face was; how dark the shadows were beneath her eyes.

Myrtale nearly turned and stalked back the way she had come. But if she did not confront the king now, it might be days before she could approach him again.

They had not seen her in the shadow of the colonnade. The morning sun had come in under the roof where the altar was; it would blind them to anything beyond.

"I can't delay him much longer," Arybbas said. "He'll be wanting an answer—and so will his king."

"You know what that answer has to be," said Nikandra. "If Macedon needs Epiros, it will come begging soon enough. You don't need to sell our niece to Philip."

"He seems honestly to want her," said Arybbas, "and she wants him. He's a good age, still young; none of his wives is as well bred as she. It's a fine match, as the world sees such things."

"That is not the world she belongs to. She is meant for other things. Higher things."

"We know what she thinks of that," Arybbas said dryly.

"Yes, you do know," said Myrtale.

It was gratifying to see how they both started and spun. She lifted her chin and fixed them both with a hard stare. "There's nothing for me here. You know that, uncle. The Mother brought me to him; now he's sent for me as he promised. What is there to think about, except how soon to send me and with how great a dowry?"

Nikandra looked ready to spit, but it was Arybbas who said, "The Mother gave you the Mysteries in their fullest strength. But they're over; he went back to his place as you went back to yours. Here is where you belong, child. If none of the Hymenides is to your liking, we'll find you another husband."

"The Mother has found me one," Myrtale said. "His ambassador is in the field, waiting for you to judge the games."

"Are you sure you want to marry Philip?" Nikandra asked.

Myrtale's eyes flashed to her. The first, heated words died unspoken. "I am sure," she said. She was proud of her calm.

The arch of Nikandra's brow made clear how easily she saw through it. "He is a manly man," she said. "A man's man, a king among men. He'll rule the world if he can. Are you strong enough to stand against him?"

"I'll stand beside him," said Myrtale.

"No woman stands beside such a man. He rules alone. Everyone—woman or man—is subject to his will."

"He knows the Mother," Myrtale said. "He worships Her."

"He uses Her as he uses everything: to gain power. I know

that kind of man, child. Are you strong enough to withstand him? Truth, now. Are you?"

"Yes," Myrtale said. "I am."

They shook their heads. They did not believe her.

To them she was only a child. She would never be more. She was not a woman; above all, she was not the Mother incarnate.

She could not tell them what she was. The law of the Mysteries forbade her.

Even for this she would not break that silence. It might not sway them in any case; they were firm in their conviction that she belonged among the sheepfolds and not in the courts of kings.

She left them to decide her fate, as they thought, between them. They could do as they pleased. And so would she.

Eleven

Myrtale could not face the queen's house just then, however welcome a refuge it had been. The games had taken over the field without: the sound of shouts and cheering echoed in the courtyards.

It was market day in the town. Myrtale let the crowd take her, drifting in its currents until she found herself outside the wall, hovering on the edge of the sacred grove.

She had never meant to come here. She turned away, perhaps too abruptly. There was nowhere to go but up: up the mountainside.

All that while, Erynna had followed without a word. Myrtale veered between resentment and gladness. As she clambered up the steep slope, following a goat-track that seemed determined to find the most difficult way and conquer it, she decided to be glad of the company. If nothing else, Erynna could catch her if she slipped.

The track doubled and veered, but after a sweating, scrambling and occasionally heart-stopping while, it rose to the summit of the ridge. The vale of Dodona spread below, the long narrow valley hemmed in by mountains with the grove and the walled town and the temple in its heart. Myrtale turned her back on it and lifted her eyes to the sky.

"Will you bring down the sun again?"

Erynna's voice startled her. She had heard it so seldom, she almost did not recognize it.

"We can draw down the moon," Erynna said, "but you outdo us all: you bring down the sun."

Myrtale's face must have been blank. Erynna grinned her sharp-toothed grin. "They sheltered you from knowledge, didn't they? Such strength; such power and glory, all gone to waste. They would mate you with a lapdog and bury you in their mountains."

"Tell me what they're afraid of," Myrtale said.

Erynna paused. She seemed slightly taken aback, but then she clapped her hands and spun on the stony height. Myrtale held her breath—the drop to either side was sheer—but Erynna's feet never touched the edge, though more than once they came close. "You," she said. "They're afraid of you. When you were born, there were portents. The sun blazed at midnight, and the stars fell in a fiery rain."

"That's not true," said Myrtale. "There were no omens at my birth. I've seen the records; I know."

"Records can be changed," Erynna said. "Truth can be forgotten. You were born to be a power in the world. Your three priestesses knew. They deliberately turned their backs on it."

Myrtale sat on what grass there was. In spite of the sun's heat, she was cold. "Why? What did they see?"

Erynna shrugged. "Power in hands other than theirs. The

end of their world. They think they can stop it with fear and ignorance. Those are poor weapons at best—and worse when that ignorance turns on all who share in it."

"Suppose you tell me what I'm ignorant of."

"A world," Erynna answered. "Have you ever wondered how you brought down the sun?"

"It was the Mother," said Myrtale, "working through me."

"The Mother is no stronger than Her instruments. Your strength is remarkable."

"Strength? For what?"

"Anything," Erynna said. "Anything at all."

It was testimony to the priestesses' teaching, or lack thereof, that Myrtale had never thought such things of herself. She was royal born, bred to serve the oracle. When she dreamed, she had dreamed of what she thought were great things: to be queen, to be mother to a king. The rest she had called nightmares: eyes watching, powers lurking, a constant sense of something just beyond the edges of her awareness.

Erynna was hinting at more. The hunger that had always been in Myrtale, that had driven her to reach higher and step farther than her elders would allow, now had a root and cause. It filled her heart so full she could hardly bear it.

"What am I?" she demanded of this stranger who seemed so wise. "What am I supposed to be?"

"What would you like to be?"

"I don't know," Myrtale said. "I was never afraid of anything, but it seems I know nothing. I can read and write Greek, I can recite the poets, I can spin and weave and do fine embroidery. I know how a queen commands her household. I've been initiated into Mysteries. A king has asked for my hand. What else is there? What other things can I be?"

"With such power as you have, lady," said Erynna, "you can stand face to face with gods. The sun is in your hand, and the moon is your servant. You can put on wings like an eagle and fly, or call to the dead and they will answer."

"May I turn men to swine, then, and set trees to dancing with the power of my voice?"

"Whatever your knowledge allows," Erynna said.

"Ah," said Myrtale. "There's the flaw in the dream. It's not all given to me out of what I am. I have to earn it."

"Isn't that true of all things worth having?"

"I suppose you can teach me," Myrtale said.

She meant to mock, but Erynna nodded, as grave as she could ever be. "I came for that. My sisters and my elders chose me, raised and taught me, to teach as much as I know. If you will learn, I have the knowledge to give."

Myrtale's heart beat hard, but her head insisted on facing a colder truth. "You're not from Macedon. You're from Thessaly. Where the witches are. Even I have heard of those."

"The world thinks it knows us," said Erynna. "That's ignorance and fear."

"A great deal of fear," Myrtale said.

Try as she would, she could not help but shiver with it. Thessaly's witches had an evil reputation.

Erynna was wicked enough, with her quick wit and her flashes of knife-edged humor, but Myrtale would not call her evil. Nor was she hideous, as her kind were said to be.

She might be a trap, and all her words and smiles might be lies. It was possible. But Myrtale was inclined to trust her. What she offered, no one had ever suggested, or hinted that it was possible.

Myrtale was hungry for it: a hunger that maybe overwhelmed caution, but she told herself she could be wary. She could take the teaching without succumbing to whatever dangers might come with it.

"I always knew," Myrtale said slowly, "that I was more than I was allowed to be. But I never imagined that I might be as much as this."

"Will you learn, then, lady?" Erynna asked. Her words were cool, but her eyes were intent. She wanted this as much as Myrtale.

That sharpened Myrtale's mistrust, but it did not turn her aside. Quite the contrary. "Whatever you have to teach," she said.

Erynna grinned and sprang.

Myrtale crouched, spun—and reached inside herself. It seemed she had all the time there was. She could see how the sun's rays struck the ground, and how the earth arched its back to receive them.

She bent the air just so, until the light turned molten and the sun's arrows made a shining wall around her. It was a beautiful and a simple thing. Surely any child could do it.

Erynna tumbled backward with a cry. The earth shifted to catch her.

She lay on the edge of the precipice, all laughter gone from her. Her eyes were open and aware; her breath came light and hard.

When Myrtale touched her, she flinched. Myrtale pulled

her back onto more solid ground. "Don't do that again," Myrtale said mildly.

Erynna shuddered so hard her teeth clacked together. "I . . . may not have as much to teach you as I thought."

"You have everything to teach me," Myrtale said. "What I did was all instinct. It needs knowledge. Skill. Discipline. I learned that in the temple; it's none the less true for that the priestesses taught me."

Erynna nodded. Her shaking had subsided. "They did train you well, all things considered. And now you know what is in you. What I have to teach, for the most part I can teach wherever we are. But for the first lessons, which are most dangerous, we had best be apart from the world."

"For how long?" said Myrtale.

"As long as necessary," Erynna answered. "A few days, we can hope."

Myrtale looked down into the valley. It seemed as if days had passed, but the sun had barely marked the passage of an hour since she began to ascend the ridge. The games below the palace wall had shifted from footraces to races on horseback. After that they would contest with weapons.

Men had a ceaseless thirst to be the best—the fastest, the strongest. Women were not supposed to care for that, not in the old world and not in this one.

Myrtale must not be a woman, then, because she wanted to be more than any woman had ever been, or any man, either. She had everything a woman had, and greatest of all, the power to bear a child. But she had a man's strength of will, or what was reckoned a man's in these days.

She turned back to Erynna. "Go. Fetch what we'll need. I'll wait for you here."

Erynna did not ask why Myrtale would not go back into Dodona. She simply nodded and began the steep descent.

Myrtale lay on the top of the world, basking like a snake in the sun. She had gone out of the queen's house to demand that her uncle give her to the Macedonian king. She still wanted that, but the world had shifted perceptibly.

She could not be among familiar people or in familiar places until she knew herself again. Nikandra had asked her if she was strong enough to hold her own against Philip. She knew she was—but here against the sky, she knew also that strength alone was not enough.

Erynna would give her what she needed. No doubt Thessaly would expect something in return. That was always so in this world or any other.

When the reckoning came, Myrtale would pay it. Maybe not as the Thessalians expected—but that would be as it would be. They were the eyes she had felt on her back all her life, the watchers in the shadows who had followed her wherever she went. They were the reason why the Mother's priestesses had raised her in ignorance, warded and shielded her so that she knew nothing of what she was.

They had been biding their time, waiting to slip beneath those walls, hoping to suborn her strength and turn it to their own purposes. That was as clear as the pattern of the games below her and the hawk's flight above.

All of them, witches and priestesses alike, had taken her for a fool—as if ignorance and innocence were the same, and stupidity ran side by side with it.

She smiled. It was not a smile any of them would have been comfortable to see. They needed her, or none would have

taken such pains either to corrupt her or to keep her from being corrupted.

She had had enough of living her life as her aunt would
wish. These people, too, might hope to use her for their own
ends. She would use them instead. She would be no one's tool,
or weapon, either.

Twelve

"Do you think she'll see sense?" Arybbas asked as Polyxena—who since she returned from Samothrace had insisted she was Myrtale—stalked off with rather impressive dignity. Troas had been teaching her to carry herself like a queen.

Nikandra had to admit she did it well. "I think Philip will be persistent. He's a man who loves to conquer women, and our niece is worth conquering. As for her . . . she'll give way in the end. It won't be easy or quick, but she's no fool, either."

"Still," Arybbas said, dithering as he too often did, "it's as good a match as this world knows. He'll treat her well for our alliance's sake, if nothing else. We'll gain much from it and lose little."

"Unless he comes to set his own man on your throne."

"That's not his way," said Arybbas.

"True enough," she said. "It's simpler to bind an ally with obligations until he's no more than a vassal. He'll do that to you."

"Maybe," Arybbas said, "and maybe I'm stronger than I look."

Nikandra hissed at him. "You're as much a fool as she is."

"I'm a king of this world," he said. "To you and your world I owe service by ancient custom, but at the day's end, I owe my first service to Epiros. Macedon offers us significant advantages in return for our niece's hand."

"All men have their weaknesses."

"As do women," he said. "Yours, sister, is to see only what will keep your world alive. Tell me the truth: whom does that profit but you?"

"It profits every woman," said Nikandra, "and every man who has a kind heart and a gentle hand."

"That's a fine dream until the armies come with fire and sword, and kill all your gentle men and rape your women. These are hard times. Our niece sees that clearly—and she is prepared to turn them to her advantage."

"She is not your property. If she belongs to anyone, it is the temple. If you have any wits at all, you will see that she marries within Epiros, and that she stays where she is safe."

"Is she really safe here?" Arybbas demanded. "Is she, sister? Won't she be more thoroughly distracted if she has a strong husband instead of the weakling you're trying to force on her? I would think you'd want her under a man's thumb, if all your fears are true and not simply a ruse to keep her in your power."

He had never come so close to defiance before. Nikandra had never pressed him so hard, either, or asked him to choose between his kingdom and his duty to the Mother.

She could press harder, but if she did, she would lose him. However aggravated she was, she did not want that. He was saying no more than she had thought for herself; though she was not about to let him know it.

She let him go, for the moment. His relief was palpable, but no less so than her own.

Nikandra chose to bury herself in duties rather than seethe in frustration. The deeper her unease, the more assiduously she fled from it, until she had almost convinced herself that there was nothing to fear.

On the third day after she had gone to the king's house, after Timarete had gone out to serve the oracle, young Attalos found her at prayer within the temple. He shuffled his feet and cleared his throat and did everything possible to draw her attention without speaking a word.

He was a rather effective distraction. She sighed heavily and rose from the floor where she had been lying on the hard-tamped earth. "Yes?" she said.

He was a gentle creature, the perfect image of a man from the old time. Just then, his humble diffidence set her teeth on edge. "Lady, if you please, the Lady Promeneia is asking for you."

Nikandra's temper did not cool at all, but she no longer cared what Attalos was or was not. Promeneia was bedridden still; the queen had sent women to look after her, and women of the town had come one by one, some to sit with her, others to offer what knowledge they had of herbs and healing.

That morning the two women who attended her had familiar faces: they were of the old families and kept as much to the old ways as they could. One sat spinning, singing softly to herself. The other knelt by the bed, where Promeneia was sitting up.

It would not be long now, Nikandra thought dispassionately.

As grimly as Promeneia clung to life, the flesh had nearly melted from her bones.

Her eyes were dark and wide. They were not seeing this world any longer, although as they turned toward Nikandra, they sparked with recognition. "Don't," she said. "Don't go after her."

Nikandra frowned. "What—"

"Don't pursue her. She'll only be more determined to thwart you."

There was no need to ask whom Promeneia meant. Everything came back to Polyxena, Myrtale, whoever and whatever she was.

"Where is she?" Nikandra asked as gently as she could manage. "What has she done?"

"Let her be," said Promeneia.

Nikandra clasped the cold, gaunt hands. "Please, lady. Tell me what you see."

"Open your eyes," Promeneia said, "and see."

"Lady, I can't—"

"Turn and look ahead," said Promeneia. "The old days are gone. The Mother gives us these to make of as we will. That child knows. She was born knowing. You have much to learn from her."

"Lady—"

"Open your eyes," Promeneia said.

The breath was leaving her. Her hands were deathly cold. Nikandra cried out to her, as if any mortal voice could stop her.

She had let go, upright as she was. The earth sighed at her leaving. Outside in the grove, the Mother's tree sang her dirge with a hundred tongues of bronze.

It was not Myrtale's fault. There was no reason for the anger that rose in Nikandra, swelling over her and breaking like a wave.

With great care she lowered the lifeless body to the bed. The two attendants looked on in shock. She who was nearer threw back her head and keened, the long wailing sound that sent a soul on its way to the Mother.

It emptied Nikandra's mind of words or thoughts or sense. There was a moment when she could have stopped it, could have brought back all the troubles that had weighed her down.

The moment passed. She gave herself up to the purity of grief.

In the face of death, time's passing had no meaning. The sun passed the zenith and set; the stars followed, and the moon on its changeful track. There were duties in the midst of it, inextricably woven with it.

For a while Nikandra forgot her troublesome niece. With Timarete she saw the rites performed and the body entrusted to the earth within the grove. There was no pyre to turn flesh and bones to ash; they buried Promeneia as she was, wrapped in a linen shroud.

No stone marked the grave. Those who attended her took care not to remember under which tree she lay. She belonged to the Mother now; her name passed to her who was now the eldest, and that name to the youngest, who had been Nikandra and was now Timarete.

There was, for now, no new Nikandra. Attalos who had served loyally since spring was male and could not take that place. Somewhere in the city or the kingdom there must be a young woman who could serve the Mother as priestesses had served Her for time out of mind.

It would not be Polyxena. She was gone, swallowed up in the woman called Myrtale, whose whole hope and ambition was to be a king's wife; and that, however it galled her aunt, was a better prospect by far than what else she might have aimed for. The new Timarete might dream of winning her back, but in the hard light of day she knew those dreams were false.

It seemed a part of those dreams, or nightmares if she would see them so, that she made her way to the Mother's tree the morning after Promeneia was laid in the earth, to find the king's messenger waiting. "Lady," the man said, "have you seen the Lady Myrtale?"

His voice tried to be empty of emotion, but Timarete's hackles rose. "How long?" she asked. "When did she go?"

The messenger looked a little startled, but then he settled: remembering what she was, no doubt. "We think six days, lady. Before the games ended, and before the Lady died."

The apprehension that Timarete had been denying uncoiled now and raised its head. Surely her vigilance had not failed so signally. Surely the gods did not mock her so.

And yet . . . "No one looked for her? No one noticed she was gone?"

"Lady," the messenger said a little desperately, "please come. The king is waiting."

Timarete did not trouble the man further. Whatever she had to ask, Arybbas would answer. And by the Mother, that answer would be to her liking, or stars would fall.

After that urgent summons, the king was not waiting when Timarete came to the palace. The queen, however, was. "They've gone hunting her," she said before Timarete could ask.

"Where do they think she's gone?"

"They're sure she's run off to Macedon," said Troas.

"Are you?"

Troas' white shoulders lifted in a shrug. "It's likely. My husband has been dragging his feet, and she's not known for her patience."

Timarete nodded. It did seem likely. But something felt odd. It might be a rumble in the earth; or it was the Mother, speaking almost too softly to be heard.

Her heart had gone still and cold. While she hid behind grief and denial, what was left of her guardianship had crumbled away. Now the girl was gone.

She had not gone alone. That understanding came too little and too late. Everything Timarete had done to prevent this had proved futile. If anything, it had made matters worse.

Whoever and whatever had taken the girl, the tides of time and fate were shifting. Whether for good or ill, Timarete could not tell—and that troubled her, too, after all her forebodings.

Surely she could not have misread the omens so badly. And yet . . .

"Will you hunt, too, aunt?" Troas asked. "I'm thinking you'll find her more easily than a pack of men in full cry."

Maybe, thought Timarete, there was nothing to fear. Maybe Myrtale had simply run off as the men believed. The Mother knew, she had done it before when she could not have her way.

But with the Macedonian envoy in Dodona, she had only to throw herself on his mercy and let him carry her off to his king. It made no sense for her to vanish without a word.

Whatever she had done, the answer was not here. "The temple needs me," Timarete said with careful coolness, "and if she wants to be found, the men will find her. Send word to me when she comes back."

"You know where she is," Troas said.

"No," said Timarete, "but the Mother does."

That was a truth so profound that it needed solitude and careful study. Timarete left too abruptly for courtesy, but Troas of all people would forgive her.

Priestesses of the grove were not forbidden to practice lesser arts than that of the oracle, but it had long been the custom that they did not stoop to such things. It was also the custom that they should learn those arts, even if they never put them to use.

Timarete had seen to it that Myrtale lived in ignorance of that whole facet of what she was. The less the girl knew, the better for them all—or so Timarete had believed.

The elder priestesses had not offered their approval, but they had not refused it, either. If they had spoken, Timarete would have schooled herself to obey.

So she told herself in the quiet of her own cell—still the same room she had lived in when she was Nikandra. The new Promeneia would need her very soon, but she could spare an hour for this.

As she walked down from the king's house, the sense of unease had grown. When she turned her mind toward Myrtale, she had found a sense of imminence, of something deep and powerful rising toward the light. What she had felt at Myrtale's birth had grown stronger—immensely so. She was not ashamed to admit that she was afraid.

Among her few belongings was a bowl carved out of alabaster, very old and very plain; it had come with the first priestesses of the grove, it was said, all the way from Egypt.

The outside was rounded to fit into cupped hands. Inside, it was polished smooth.

She folded back the linen wrappings, then filled the bowl almost to the brim with water from the Mother's stream. She lit the lamp and hung it above, where it cast light but no glare on the water.

She drew a deep breath and closed her eyes. All her power was given to the oracle. When she diverted it, she had to quell the surety that if she let it go, it would run wild.

She could control it. She opened her eyes and looked down into the pale shimmer of the scrying bowl.

It was slow, but she had expected that. Magic blurred the sight. The stronger the magic, the harder it was to force it into focus.

Myrtale's magic was very strong. For a long while there was only a dazzle of light. Then, little by little, a vision took shape.

It looked like a goat pasture, high and stony, with patches of grass and scrub and thorny bushes. A stream ran through it. Myrtale knelt by the water, washing what must be her only garment: she was naked and her hair was loose.

Timarete did not recognize the little dark woman who splashed in the stream, but there was no mistaking the aura that radiated from her. It was crimson and black and royal purple, and spoke of a multitude of dark things.

"Thessaly," Timarete hissed. She caught herself before she spat in the water and broke the vision.

That much she had allowed Myrtale to learn: that the witches of Thessaly were dangerous. They followed a dark path, sacred to the deep powers and the gods below. Their worship was of the Mother, that was true, but it lived on Her left hand, in blood and endless night.

Timarete cursed herself now for a thrice and ten times fool. In all her years of guarding the girl, protecting her against any power that might rouse the dangers Timarete had foreseen, she had detected no sign of this particular threat.

She had looked for it. She had cast her spells toward Thessaly, as toward many other places of power in this world. She had searched out every cranny, and found only emptiness. The one enemy she had to fear, or so she had thought, was Myrtale herself.

The witches were great diviners and even greater deceivers. They would know what Myrtale was—and of course they would have come looking for her, now that she had escaped her aunt's vigilance. She had power they would lust after, and she would know no better than to trust them.

It was like their wickedness to slither in when Timarete was most direly distracted. For all she knew, they had tempted Myrtale into releasing her power, and so brought about Promeneia's death.

Timarete called herself to order. Maybe it had not gone too far yet. The witch with Myrtale was young; she must be the bait to draw the quarry in.

No doubt she would be teaching Myrtale simple arts to amaze her untaught mind. The other arts, greater and more perilous, would wait until the snare was set.

Timarete let the vision open before her. The two young women could be anywhere in the mountains, but she did not think they had gone very far—not on foot. Myrtale had been living in the palace; her body had softened into an image of this new world's womanhood. Even the hardened soles of her feet had been rubbed and scraped and oiled until they were judged fit to walk on polished pavements.

The shape of the hillside above them struck a chord of familiarity. Timarete peered closer. Just as she began to think she knew the place, Myrtale looked up, full into her eyes, and bared her teeth in a she-wolf's grin.

The vision winked out. Timarete stared down into blank and faintly shimmering water.

Through the anger and frustration she allowed a flicker of respect. It took more than strength to play that game. However she had gained it, Myrtale had a little skill.

But Timarete was older and wiser, and now she was forewarned. She held in memory the long bare hill with its jagged crown, and the angle of the sun down its slope.

She could write it and draw it and send the message to the king and his hunters. That would be the wise thing. But it well might send the quarry to ground; then no one would find her.

Timarete had not gone hunting in time out of mind, but she had not forgotten the way of it. She found the tunic in her chest of belongings, the high-laced sandals and the woolen cloak that could be a blanket at need. She hesitated over the bow and quiver, but in the end she took them, first making sure the string was fresh and the arrows well-fletched and straight.

With a bag of cheese and bread and a skin of wine, she reckoned herself ready. The new Promeneia was still serving the oracle; Attalos went about his morning duties, which kept him well away from Timarete.

She paused. This might be madness. She had power, but Myrtale had more than that. If she had awakened, with as little art as she could possibly have, she was deadly dangerous.

Timarete was strong enough. She had to trust in that.

Thirteen

The hunt was up. Both bait and diversion had succeeded; Timarete was running straight toward the trap.

Myrtale indulged in a moment of guilt and superstitious fear. Timarete was, after all, her aunt; it was ill luck in Thessaly as in Epiros to shed kindred blood.

Myrtale hardened her heart. Timarete deserved this comeuppance for what she had done to Myrtale in the name of gods knew what. If the Mother took umbrage, then so be it. Because of Timarete, Myrtale was barely creeping toward knowledge; her destiny was perilously far away.

She had to seize it soon, before it was too late. She had to claim the magic she was born for. Timarete would stop her if she could—and that must not happen.

The Mother would forgive. Myrtale laid the last snare, surrounding that high and distant goat pasture with a web of subtle spells.

To the eye it was an oddity of colored and colorless threads, tangled together on a scrap of woven wool. It looked like the remnants of a clumsy child's embroidery. Each strand alone was a tiny thing, but all together they could trap and hold a god—and that, for all her pretensions, Timarete was not.

Erynna was already gone, making her way into the high places. There against the sky, Myrtale could claim a fuller power—and if she wished, draw down the moon.

But first they must be rid of Timarete. She came on with gratifying if slightly alarming speed. Myrtale hastened to weave the last of the spells.

She bound the last knot and bit it off with her teeth. A slight shock ran through her; she started and nearly dropped the weaving. Hastily she thrust it into the purse she wore at her belt.

It buzzed there like a swarm of bees. It could sting, too, if she let it go. She shuddered in her skin.

Magic was no easy thing to master. Even this little working, so simple any hedge-witch could do it, made her dizzy and sapped her strength. She staggered as she turned in the direction that Erynna had gone.

By an effort of will she made herself walk steadily, firm and not too fast, up the track toward the summit. She fought the urge to run—if she had, she would have fallen. Timarete was almost within sight.

The spell was reaching already to tangle the priestess' feet. It tugged at Myrtale's own, but she pulled herself free.

Erynna waited just below the summit, where a hollow hid her from sight but let her see what passed below. She had made herself a cradle of thread and trapped a ray of sunlight in it.

The thread was smoldering. Myrtale spoke a word that brought a drop of rain to quench the fire.

Erynna's glance was unreadable. She was not jealous,

surely. Her arts were far superior to Myrtale's and might always be.

Without warning the witch left the hollow, slipping away down the slope. A fold of ridge there concealed her from the trap.

Myrtale wanted very much to see Timarete stumble into the snare, but she had to admit that Erynna was wise. Grudgingly but quickly, she followed where Erynna led.

Timarete was hot and breathless with climbing. Her skin prickled as she came up the last ascent and looked down into the pasture.

It was empty. She could not have said she was surprised. She paused to breathe, leaning on a stone.

The girl could not have gone far. Witches in Thessaly could fly, but there was no sign or smell of the ointment. For whatever reason, Myrtale's new teacher elected to travel as mortals did.

Timarete began the descent into the pasture. It was much longer and steeper than it had looked. So long and steep in fact that she began to suspect a trap.

It was clever, she thought when she tried to pause and found she could not. The path went on and on, winding like a tangle of thread. No matter how far she walked, she advanced neither forward nor back.

She set her teeth and pushed against the spell. It was well made. It did not yield.

She was not afraid, not yet. A body could die in such a trap. But she had arts of her own. She would work free of the spell; she would win her way home.

Eventually. Somewhat before her feet had worn raw with

walking forever without advancing, and her flesh had melted from her bones with hunger and exhaustion.

Not only Myrtale could lay a trap. She followed Erynna innocently round a bend in the path and walked straight into a camp of armed men.

As soon as she realized what she had done, she spun on her heel and bolted. A man who seemed as tall and wide as the Mother's temple barred her way. He grunted as she collided with him, but he barely swayed.

She knew no spell swift enough to free her before he held her fast. He was adept at restraining small, snapping, clawing beasts. In half a dozen breaths he held her motionless, breathing hard, glaring through tangled hair at the king's envoy of Macedon.

Lagos' face was carefully expressionless. "Lady," he said. "We're most glad to have found you."

Myrtale was anything but glad to have found him. This time when she twisted in her captor's grip, he let her go except for a light but firm clasp on one wrist. She chose to ignore that, glaring past him at Erynna.

The witch looked back at her without guilt. "Why?" Myrtale asked her.

"It's time," she answered.

Myrtale tossed her head in fierce denial. "We were not finished!"

"For now we are," said Erynna.

Myrtale bit her lips hard. Maybe this was not a betrayal. Maybe it was a gift.

She wanted Philip still, his kingdom and the power that came with them both. She wanted magic, too, as much as her hands could grasp. Erynna had as much as promised her that she could have it all.

She would trust the witch, for the moment. She turned back toward Lagos. "You were hunting me?"

"We had thought you missing, lady," he said.

"That I was not," said Myrtale, "but I thank you for your diligence."

"Epiros will owe Macedon a debt," he said. "Perhaps, lady, you can suggest a way in which his majesty may repay us."

Myrtale had not heard that the lords of Macedon were skilled in the intrigues of courts, but this was as subtle as anything in the queen's house of Epiros. Lagos had just offered her what she had professed to want. Arybbas would not refuse Philip's suit, not if Philip's envoy brought back the wayward bride.

Her belly clenched. It was one thing to want and fret and dream. It was another to take what was offered, that was everything she had wanted, and yet—

She nodded crisply. "I can think of a payment for the debt. Take me to my uncle."

She held her breath. A queen learned to be imperious, but men did not always do as they were told.

It seemed Lagos had been raised properly. He bowed to her will.

Fourteen

Myrtale returned to Dodona on the back of a Macedonian warhorse, with the king's envoy beside her. Rumor had it that she had run off to marry the king in spite of her kin.

Neither Lagos nor Myrtale did anything to quell the rumor. She was amused to see how furious her uncle was, but how powerless he was to speak of it.

Completely without intending it, she had won the battle. Arybbas had no choice but to give her what she asked.

She spared little thought for Timarete. Her aunt would escape the spell—but not, by the Mother, easily or quickly. By the time she roared off the mountain in a fiery trail of outrage, Myrtale would be long gone.

That was no more than she deserved. She was fortunate that Myrtale had done no worse.

Lagos was in no way reluctant to end his embassy. He had his king's inclination toward swift action, and this had taken more than long enough, in his estimation.

Myrtale was of entirely the same persuasion. Her sister would have delayed them all for at least a handful of days, to gather the following proper to a king's bride. But Myrtale had waited too long as it was.

The day after she returned from the mountain, she rode out of the king's house. The sky was grey and blustery, shot with sudden, dazzling flashes of sunlight. Summer though it still was, winter's breath had chosen to blow—just a little; enough to remind every mortal that neither warmth nor brightness would long endure.

Nor would dark or cold. It was all one in the Mother. Time passed in its endless round, from light to dark and back to light again.

She shook off such thoughts. Now of all days, she should think only of the light. She was going to be married to the Bull of Minos, the Lion of Macedon, the king who alone was worthy of her.

For all Troas' protestations, Myrtale took with her a caravan of treasures fit for a queen, a train of royal gifts, a company of the king's guards, and a pair of tattooed Thracian slaves, each leading one of the great hounds of Molossia. For herself Myrtale brought little: her young snake in its basket, a chest of belongings, and Philip's gift, the witch Erynna.

Erynna had returned to her old silence. Myrtale did not choose to break it. She disliked to be taken by surprise, even if that ambush led to her heart's desire.

That heart of hers was trying to play her false. It kept beating wildly and then going cold.

When she left Dodona for Samothrace, she had known she was coming back—even if she cherished some hope she might not be. This was a truer parting. Even if she came back, it would never be the same. She would return as a wife and, gods willing, a queen.

In the crowded solitude of a royal bride's train, she ran over in memory the lessons she had learned on the mountain. There was more to them—much more; but she refused to beg Erynna for them. Erynna would teach them, Myrtale did not doubt, but in her own time and at her own pace.

Myrtale could wait her out. Meanwhile there was a new country to see and new faces to remember, and a new world opening before her.

And Philip. She had, like a child, half hoped he would be waiting at the border of his country. There were men waiting, but they were not the king—only the king's Companions, sent as an escort.

That was a considerable honor. It was not enough. Philip might think he had her, but he would learn what was worthy of her.

His men were bold: they looked her full in the face. It seemed they found her beautiful, though she heard them talking in their own language that was not quite the one spoken in the peasants' huts of Epiros. They called her a foreigner, and muttered of proper Macedonian brides.

She smiled at them, aiming to addle their poor male wits. For many that was enough. The rest she wooed with words, quick brushes of attention, learning each man's name and family and whether he had wife or lover. And sons—they did love to talk of their sons.

While she spoke to them, she softened her accent—not so much that she could be accused of pretending to be Macedonian, but enough to seem less jarringly foreign. Not every man was so easily won over, but she had gained no enemies, either.

It was ten days' journey at the pace of an oxcart from Dodona to Pella. That was time enough for Myrtale to weigh and measure Philip's men and discover their names and families and where they came from. They were shy at first, but when she persevered, they proved willing enough to speak to her, though they had not decided, yet, to accept her.

Erynna kept to herself. Her escort, Epirote and Macedonian alike, knew what she was: Myrtale caught the glances and the muttered words. They did not appear to know that she was Myrtale's teacher, or else they chose not to acknowledge that uncomfortable fact. Myrtale, it seemed, was not to suffer for their misunderstanding of Erynna's nation and arts.

Was it a misunderstanding? Myrtale slid away from the thought. In those few days on the mountain, she had opened her eyes to a whole new world.

It was still there, all around her. Every ray of sunlight and every shadow under the moon held both spirit and power. It was numinous, the Mother's priestesses would say— Promeneia most of all. She had seen more clearly than the others.

It was all one in the Mother. Myrtale held tightly to that, and made it her constant prayer. Inside herself she felt the power growing and putting forth roots, making itself part of this land into which she traveled.

It was not so different at first from her wild mountain kingdom, a land of high pastures and steep rocky slopes and sudden cataracts. Then as they drew near the king's city, the mountains opened into a rolling plain cut through with rivers and, on the far horizon, the glimmer of a lake.

There was Philip's city, the place where he was born, royal Pella. It stood on the shores of the lake: a walled city that dwarfed Dodona. The sprawling edifice on the hill above it must be his palace, and that too was greater than any she had seen.

It seemed forever that they traversed the plain, crawling infinitesimally closer to the city and the palace. Myrtale was put in mind, with a stab of guilt and a prickle of fear, of the spell she had laid on Timarete.

Surely the priestess had escaped by now and was back in her temple. Equally surely Myrtale would come to the city before the sun set; it was only morning, and the men and horses were fresh, with the smell of home in their nostrils.

This would be home, she promised herself. On this day it was almost unbearably strange. She clutched her little snake's basket for comfort, and looked up at the palace walls and tried to remember the pride and strength that had brought her here.

This palace was worthy of her. Whether she would be worthy of it . . .

She would be. She was. She raised her chin and sat straight on the bay horse's back.

The beast caught the spark from her, arched its neck and danced—gently, but it made her smile. Grins flashed through her escort.

That little bit of insouciance had done more to win them over than all her careful blandishments. Macedonians liked bravura. She would have to remember that.

Fifteen

Once Lagos' embassy passed the gates of Pella, Myrtale expected to be taken directly to the palace. Instead she found herself in a house of no distinction without and breathtaking luxury within, under the hands of half a dozen diligent servants. Her baggage and its treasures were gone, her maid and her escort taken off wherever servants went when they were not guarding royal brides.

She was alone in a house full of strangers. They stripped her naked and had at her with clippers and tweezers and pastes, stripping every hair off her body that was not on her head, then rubbing her with sweet oils and scraping them off with strigils. They followed that with water, hot and then cold, that bore with it an indefinable scent of the sacred, and vigorous scrubbing with bundles of herbs that overcame the reek of the oil with their sweet, sharp fragrance.

At first Myrtale struggled, startled; she squawked indecorously. But the servants had iron hands and no mercy. Eventually she judged it best to grit her teeth and submit.

She had never been so vehemently clean. Her skin felt

strange, as smooth and soft as a newborn's. She stung in her tenderest parts.

They washed her hair in herbs and henna and dried it with Egyptian linen, then brushed it until it shone. They painted her face and her fingertips and toes, and hung her with heavy ropes of gold and amber, emerald and ruby and carnelian.

Just as she thought she would go before the people wearing nothing but her hair and a king's treasure, they dressed her in an elaborately embroidered gown of imperial purple bound with a golden girdle, adorned her feet with golden sandals, and crowned her with gold and laid over it the wedding veil. Her skirts were so stiff she could barely move, but that was no impediment to these servants. They half-carried her out of the room.

In the central court of the house, an altar stood. Victims waited for the sacrifice: a snow-white kid for Artemis, to whom Myrtale must dedicate the girdle she had so recently been given; a pair of white doves for Aphrodite; and for Hera, a cream-colored heifer. They regarded Myrtale with calm and innocent eyes.

The court was full of people—but not of Philip. In his place stood Lagos, speaking for his king here as he had in Epiros.

Myrtale stood firm against the rising of anger. This was not her father's house, either, and the grave-faced woman who assisted her was not her mother, as tradition would have dictated. It was all for show, to make a marriage that the Mother had long since made in the Mysteries on Samothrace.

She spoke the words as she was bidden, slit the victims' throats with fast, firm strokes and poured out the blood in the Mother's honor. It was all the Mother, always, here as everywhere.

From the sacrifice she passed to the feast. In this unfamiliar hall, among all these unfamiliar faces, she sat enthroned on a golden chair, swathed in her veils, and watched a crowd of strangers eat and drink and dance and make merry.

She ate nothing. There was wine that she was required to drink, but she barely sipped it. Her stomach was an aching knot.

The man who sat beside her was not her husband. If he came to her bed tonight, she would kill him. She made that decision calmly and reasonably, without resort to temper.

Meanwhile she endured a wedding feast without a bridegroom, and waited for the hours to pass. Men in Epiros were fond of their wine, but Macedonians could down a vat of it and still be steady on their feet.

Under cover of the veil, she wove stray threads and bits of hair into a certain shape. She let it rest in her hand, keeping the words inside until she should need them.

This place, this country, was full of magic. Strange that she should become aware of it in the midst of a raucous feast. It was deep and quiet beneath, flowing up through her feet like sap through the roots and veins of the Mother's tree. In this very mortal celebration, she felt the Mother's hand, subtle yet strong.

The long day waned. The feast wound to its ending. When the guests rose, Myrtale restrained herself from leaping up with them. Strong men lifted her, chair and all, and carried her back out to the court.

The wedding carriage was waiting. Rather than mules or oxen, snow-white mares drew it. It was made of rare woods from the east, sweetly scented and richly carved; its fastenings were all of gold, and the mares' trappings were plated with the bright metal.

Myrtale stiffened against the hands that lifted her into it, but they did not belong to Lagos. They were not Philip's, either. Strangers raised her, nobles by the richness of their dress; later she would learn their names. For now she committed their faces to memory.

In this strange wedding, she had yet to show her own face to any of them, or unveil herself before the bridegroom. Nor would she until she stood face to face with her proper husband.

The torches were lit. The dancers had come out, and the players on flute and drum and lyre. One of the white mares pawed imperiously.

Myrtale's patience snapped. She wrested the reins from the man who held them, tipped him out of the cart, and turned the mares toward the open gate.

They needed no encouragement. Torchbearers scattered. Dancers fled. The marriage hymn ended on a broken note.

If that was an omen, so be it. Myrtale had had enough. She did not know this city, but the way was clear inside her, as if someone had cast a spell to draw her to her desire.

The spellweaving was still in her hand. Maybe she would not need it, but she made no move to cast it away.

She rode the cart like a chariot, streaming smoke and fire from the torches, down the processional way and then up toward the palace.

Its gate was open. Torches burned there, and a crowd waited.

Myrtale saw one face only out of them all. He stood in the middle, dressed in purple and gold, foursquare and sturdy but oddly graceful.

She aimed the mares straight toward him. People scattered; he stood his ground. She brought the mares to a rearing halt full in front of him, gentled them down and saw them settled while he stood watching with his face gone blank.

When they were still but for heaving sides and flaring nostrils, she lifted the veil and let it fall.

She heard his breath catch. She was careful not to let him see her smile. If he had thought he was going to slip her in and hide her in his harem as if he had been the Great King of Persia, she had put an end to that in front of half of Pella.

She stood in the cart, bright-lit in torchlight, and let him choose his course. He could turn his back on her and repudiate her, and she could not say a word.

Or he could stride up to her and reach out his hands and lift her down. The heat of him was just as she remembered, the strength that never wavered under her weight, the clean male smell that was part leather and part bronze and part horse, underlaid with musk and smoke and sweat. No effete perfumes here, though the scent of the garland he wore was sharply sweet.

It was bay, and in his hand he held another: Aphrodite's own myrtle, such as she had worn in the Mysteries.

He laid aside her crown of gold and crowned her with myrtle, naming her with it, then sealing the naming with a long, thirsty kiss.

She remembered little of the passage from the gate to the bridal chamber. There was music and dancing and song, and there were words spoken and promises made. They meant little beside the warmth of her hand in his, and his presence beside her.

It was all a part of him, this whole kingdom, all these people and this palace and this earth they danced upon. When she took his hand, all of it became hers.

They were bound in the Mother and the Mystery. Now they proclaimed the great marriage for the world to see.

The door was shut. The bed was laid for them, strewn with petals and fragrant herbs. A cluster of lamps burned with a steady light.

People were singing outside, dancing and playing on drums and cymbals. The sounds were faint through the heavy door, dim and far away.

Philip stood just inside the door, shifting from foot to foot. "You're afraid," Myrtale said as the truth came to her. "This thing between us—it terrifies you."

"Yes." It was a lion's growl. "I've never run away from anything in my life."

"I don't see you running now," she said.

"There's half a hundred howling roisterers out there," said Philip. "I'd be torn limb from limb."

She knew better than to laugh. As little as she had been taught of men, this she knew: they were terribly tender when it came to their dignity.

She let fall her swathings of garments and stood dressed only in gold and her hair. "Come here," she said.

He shuddered as he drew in a breath. She crossed the room in a long, smooth stride and took his hands. They were cold.

She warmed them against her breasts. They opened as if of their own accord. She smiled up at him.

She watched the fear leave him. A woman in his hands he understood—almost as well as war or kingship.

For her it was not so familiar a thing, but this man she

knew. She had known him even before she saw him in the Mysteries, deep down in her heart. He was the one the Mother had made for her.

He swept her up just as she leaped into his arms. Then she felt safe to laugh. The sound vanished in his own roar of relief and sudden joy.

Sixteen

Myrtale's body ached in very pleasurable ways. Philip had fallen asleep as men did, sprawled across the tumbled bed. She pushed him over to make room for herself; he muttered and scowled but did not wake.

She propped herself on her elbow and rested her eyes on him. His body in the lamplight was black-furred and white-skinned and strong. She traced lines of scars: down along his side, deep-sunken in his thigh, and thin pale slashes along his arms and the backs of his hands.

Her own hands were childishly smooth beside his. Her calluses from labor in the temple were fading; his were set hard, marks of sword and spear and bow. His palms were broad but his fingers long; one had been broken and set crooked.

She laid words of guard and blessing on him, running her hands over his body, kissing each gate of the soul. There were maybe not so many of those as she chose to find.

When she reached the eyes, they were open. She had heard no change in his breathing and sensed no sign of waking, but he was awake and aware of her. She smiled and kissed his eyelids and said, "Good morning, husband."

"It's morning already?"

His growl made her laugh. "Nearer dawn than sunset," she said, "but a fair while till sunrise."

"Were you casting spells on me?"

"Blessings," she said.

He frowned. She stroked his brow smooth. "I am the Mother's child. All women are. She blesses me; I pass it on to you."

He did not look as if he quite believed her, but he let go his tension. When she took him inside her, he was ready: startled at first, then eager.

"You aren't used to a woman who takes a man," she said.

He was falling asleep again, but he shook himself awake. "You come on like an army," he said, "storming the barricades."

"And you don't?"

He lifted himself on his elbows. She lay on her side, watching him. He was dangerous as any animal is, simmering with barely controlled violence.

She could bring down the sun. What was a king of men to that?

He met her eyes and held, but she saw what it cost him. Deliberately she softened her stare. His hackles went down; his breath came less sharp.

He tossed his head. "Gods, woman! Make you a man and put you in armor and you'd be Achilles himself."

"That sulky child?" She lay back, well aware of his eyes as they traveled down her body. "He died a fool's death. Odysseus, now—he had wits as well as brawn. *He* won Troy."

"So he did," Philip said. "Got his own epic, too. But when people dream of heroes, it's Achilles they want most to be."

"I don't," she said. "I don't think you do, either. You can fight—better than most, I'm told. But you're best at the council table, or moving men to do your will through words rather than blows. You'll make Macedon a power in the world, but you won't do that simply by throwing armies against it."

"Armies have their place," he said. "I'll make ours the best there is. But they're expensive. If I can get what I need by sitting at a table and talking, I'll do it. As long as the men across from me know I've got a few thousand spears to back me up, they'll listen."

"You're a man after Odysseus' heart," she said.

"Not Agamemnon?"

"A coward and a braggart, who bullied others into fighting his war for him. I don't see him in you."

"You are a woman of decided opinions," Philip said.

He was more amused than not. His fear had faded. He was beginning to look at her as a human creature instead of a dream or a nightmare.

"I know what I want," she said. "I do my best to take it."

"You should have been a man," he said.

"Why would I want that?"

She had taken him aback. "A man is— A woman—"

"Ask yourself," she said, "why a woman has to be weak to make a man feel strong. Are men so weak that women's strength is a threat to them?"

"So it is true," he said. "You're one of the old kind. I thought they were gone from the world."

"Not yet," she said.

She had meant to protest that she was no such thing, but the words would not come out. She would not be what her aunt had raised her to be, but she could not be a submissive woman of this age, either. She was the child of her blood after all, for all her struggles against it.

She watched him to see what he would do. For a long while he simply watched her in return. She had shocked the sleep out of him: his eyes were clear.

She was nodding off herself when he reached for her. His hand closed around her throat.

That woke her, but she felt no fear. He was testing. He might kill her; he might die first. It was all in the Mother's hands.

Gently but firmly, she closed her own fingers around his testicles. She did not squeeze, any more than he squeezed her throat. She smiled.

She felt the gust of fury in him. Then suddenly he laughed. He fell backward, shaking with it, so long and hard he hiccoughed into silence.

Her grip turned from threat to caress. His phallus stiffened. He groaned, but he made no move to escape.

Never be predictable. That had been Troas' advice. She had said it would catch a man's attention, and that did seem to be true.

It was a terribly easy thing to do. Having teased him until he begged for mercy, she left him lying and pretended to fall asleep.

He was no fool. He surged up over her and caught her in his arms and thrust so deep she cried out, half in pain and half in pleasure.

Her nails raked his back. He bucked and cursed. She bit his ear until she tasted blood, locked her legs around his middle and trapped him as he had trapped her.

Love was a sickness, the poets said. It possessed the spirit; it drove men mad.

Myrtale reveled in it. Her body ached and burned and sang. When they had fought this last battle to a roaring conclusion, she fell back panting, running with sweat, grinning at her glorious brute of a husband.

He grinned back. The sullenness was stripped from him. He had loosed the tight control he kept on himself; he let her see what he was inside, the wild boy whom she had always known was there.

That was the Philip she loved. She swore an oath to herself to keep that boy alive no matter how old or jaded the man grew. For her he would always be young and light of heart.

Morning took both of them by surprise. They had fallen asleep in one another's arms. When the door burst open and a cheering crowd poured in, Philip surged up with a roar.

Myrtale, less warlike, still was directly behind him, armed for battle. She met eyes both strange and familiar and stared them down. Men blushed; women drew back.

They looked so abashed that she could not help but laugh. "Come in!" she said. "Be welcome. Feast with us."

They had come to sweep the bride and groom away; instead they found themselves borne off to the wedding feast. Then for a little while Myrtale and Philip were alone again, until the servants came to bathe and dress them.

There was too little time for anything but a kiss. Myrtale took full advantage of it. It might have led to more, if they had not been invaded by an army of faithful servitors.

Seventeen

For three days Philip celebrated his marriage to the princess from Epiros. On the fourth, he had to be king again. And Myrtale had to face the reality of the bargain she had made.

When he left her on that fourth morning, the servants who had attended her through the wedding were not in evidence. In their place came an elderly woman, thin and erect, who looked Myrtale up and down with an expression of barely concealed disdain. She performed the service of a maid, making it clear that this was not her wonted duty, nor did she intend to make a habit of it.

The clothes in which she dressed Myrtale were rich enough, and the ornaments that went with them were the king's gift, fit for a queen. In soft new wool and heavy gold and plates of amber, Myrtale followed the stiff-backed servant out of the wedding chamber into the depths of the women's quarters.

These were small rooms but richly painted, with floors of figured stone and furnishings of rare cedar and cypress inlaid with gold and ivory. The innermost was adorned with images of nymphs and satyrs dancing in a landscape of hills and streams and feathery-branched trees. "This is yours," the servant said in an accent that Myrtale had learned to recognize as high-bred Macedonian.

Maybe the woman was not a servant. Maybe she was something more. Myrtale could hardly ask without giving insult.

She could ask the more immediate question. "Mine? My room?"

"Yours," said the old woman.

Myrtale turned slowly. Amid the treasure of painted walls, she had almost failed to see the bed—barely wide enough for two—and the chest at its foot and the table beside it, and the cluster of lamps that lit the windowless space. Apart from its walls, it was nearly as ascetic as her cell in Dodona's temple.

"This is not where the king sleeps," she said.

The old woman's eyes were hooded, her face unreadable. "The king sleeps where he pleases. This is your place."

"Mine? Will my women share it?"

"You belong to the king now," her guide said.

"And my maid belongs to me," said Myrtale. She did her best to speak coolly, as if it did not matter. "Fetch her, if you please."

The old woman bowed, a bare dip of the head, and left Myrtale standing among the painted dancers.

Myrtale was prepared to wait for as long as it took. She investigated the chest and found her belongings in it, with an armful of folded gowns and mantles that looked newly made, and a box of jewels into which her golden ornaments fit exactly.

Her snake in its basket was nowhere in the room. She had hardly spared it a thought through the wedding, but now she was alone, she missed it. If it had been cast away or lost, she would turn the palace on its head until she found it.

She had thought she was calm, but her body would not sit still. She kilted up her skirts and ventured out of the room.

There was no lock on the door and no barrier beyond. She was not a prisoner. She followed the currents of air past closed doors and silent rooms to blinding light.

As her eyes adapted to the glare, she saw that she was in a courtyard, and the courtyard was full of women. Those in the colonnade were doing familiar things: spinning, weaving, embroidery. Those in the open space brought Myrtale to a wide-eyed halt.

There were half a dozen of them, more or less. They were dressed in short chitons tight-bound across the breasts. Most practiced archery, shooting arrows at targets down the length of the courtyard. One or two vied with javelins.

Much about this palace was unexpected; after the rumors of a nation of shepherds and cattle-herders sharing the byres with their livestock, she had found order and beauty and luxury that outshone anything she had known in Epiros. But this startled her speechless.

Philip's women trained like men. She began to wonder if he had been mocking her when they lay together, wondering at her strength and seeming astonished that she would speak to him as an equal. His own palace was full of warrior women.

So much for her aunt's conviction that she had sold herself in slavery to a man. This was the Mother's country—she had felt it from the moment she passed its borders. Here were the Mother's daughters, skilled in war and the hunt.

As Myrtale stared, one of the javelin-throwers saluted an especially skillful cast with a whoop, a dance, and a swoop toward the colonnade, where a plump maid played with a toddling child. The child sprang into the woman's arms; she laughed and spun him about.

She was a slender woman, tall and reddish-fair. The child was stocky and sturdy, with a shock of black curls. There was no mistaking where he came from.

Myrtale's belly knotted. In the men's world, the queen was the heir's mother. If Philip had a son, healthy and strong and bright-eyed as this one seemed to be, then this lithe young woman must be queen of Macedon.

Myrtale had come to be queen. She had not allowed herself to think that there might be one in place already. It was meant that she hold that office.

Her sister wife bounced the child on her hip and smiled, all bright innocence. "Good morning! Welcome to our symposium. Did you sleep well? Have you eaten?"

Myrtale realized that her mouth was open. She shut it.

Others had gathered, eyeing her with interest or curiosity, but no enmity that she could detect. Were they all that ingenuous here? Or did they simply have no need to be suspicious?

"My name is Philinna," the young mother said. "Audata is there"—she pointed with her chin at one of the archers—"and Phila is weaving the war-cloak yonder."

Myrtale dipped her head to each of her sister wives. They regarded her without either anger or suspicion, though Phila seemed slightly wary. Philinna was too full of her son and her delight in the day to see past her own self-satisfaction.

Whatever envy might rankle in them, they were not showing it to Myrtale. It must be there; they would not be human if it had not been.

Women learn to love their slavery. Myrtale's aunt had told her that. It gave her an odd sensation in her gut to find herself agreeing with it.

She put on a smile. She would never consent to be enslaved, but she could discipline herself to live with her fellow wives. "I'm honored to meet you all," she said. "They call me Myrtale; I come from Epiros."

"Dodona, yes," Philinna said: "where the oracle is. It is true you were to be one of the priestesses?"

Myrtale held tightly to her smile. "I was," she said. "Will you show me your palace? I've only a seen a little of it. Are we allowed to go everywhere in it? Are there interesting hiding places?"

She had judged rightly: Philinna was young enough to nod eagerly. She handed her son back to his nurse, brushing a kiss over his hair. He fussed at leaving her, but quieted as the nurse thrust an ample breast at him.

He caught hold with the air of a conquering king. As Philinna led Myrtale out of the court, the sound of his sucking was loud in the silence.

Philinna did not let that last long. Well before they slipped through a door near the end of the colonnade, she had filled the air with chatter.

It was bright, entertaining, and all but devoid of useful substance. Myrtale did gain from it that the child's name was Arrhidaios; that he was two summers old; and that Audata, who as yet was as lissome as a warrior woman should be, was expecting a child in the spring. Myrtale also learned that Audata was overly fond of honey in all its forms, Phila thought bows and javelins were excessively manly, and Philinna had a team of chariot horses whom she loved to drive on the plain below the city.

"You'll have to come with me," she said. "We have races. My mares always win. It makes the men chew their beards, they get so angry. *They* have to drive stallions, you know. Which is all very well, but stallions are so easily distracted."

"So are men," Myrtale said, for once getting a word in.

Philinna laughed, a ringing peal that echoed in the corridor. As far as Myrtale could tell, they were walking from end to end of the women's quarters, down toward the public gate. A handful of servants passed by with all the makings of a bath: heavy bronze basin, cloths and jars and oil scrapers, and ewers of steaming water.

"Someone's taking a bath on the men's side," Philinna observed. "He must be getting married, or else being buried. They don't trouble with it otherwise."

"The king does," said Myrtale.

"Ah," said Philinna with a lift and shake of the shoulders. "He's different. The others aren't exactly howling savages, but they have their ways. He wants them all to be more Greek."

"Do they object?"

"Some do. Some see what he's trying to do. We can fight together, you see. The Greeks squabble constantly among their tribes and cities. With a strong enough army, we can roll right over them, take their cities and teach them to be a single nation with a single king."

Myrtale regarded her in increased respect. For all her wide eyes and her bright young voice, she was clearly educated. She could think.

Aloud Myrtale said, "Our husband is ambitious."

"Aren't you?" said Philinna.

That set Myrtale back on her heels. "Of course."

"So are we all," Philinna said. "We didn't all choose to be here, but it's a good place to be—a strong place. We'll go far with Philip to lead us."

"You'd fight beside him? He'd let you?"

Philinna shrugged. "Who's to say he won't? He likes his women strong—like his men; like his country."

He might stop short of sending his queen to battle, but Myrtale kept the thought to herself. They had come to the corridor's end, where a door opened on a place both strange and startlingly familiar.

Unlike the sharp-cornered boxes of rooms and courtyards elsewhere in the palace, this room was round, like a temple of the old ways. A dome hung in the air above it, open at the zenith to let a shaft of sunlight down to the bare stone floor. Heavy pillars held up the roof; the walls beyond were painted, but in an older style than in the women's rooms.

Here was an altar and an image of Herakles in his lionskin, carved in marble in the manner of the Greeks. Away in the shadows, a far more ancient shape squatted, watching over the shrine that had begun as Hers and would continue to be so beneath the words and rites of the men's upstart gods.

As Myrtale paused beside Philinna just inside the doorway, a sinuous shape slithered across the floor. Two others followed it: one somewhat smaller and one hardly larger than a hatchling.

The Mother's snakes coiled around her feet and explored upward. Her own, her hatchling with its darker scales and narrower head, came to her hand; as she lifted it to her breast, it kissed her face with the soft tickle of its tongue before it slid into the fold of her chiton.

Its weight was welcome, its presence reassuring in ways she felt no need to explain. She breathed easier for knowing it was here and safe and protected in the Mother's care.

Philinna's eyes were wide. "So it's true," she said. "You *are* a snake witch. My grandmother used to tell me stories. They ruled long ago, before the warrior kings came."

Myrtale opened her mouth to deny she was a witch, but she could hardly do that. Instead she said, "Where I come from, the old ways are still alive."

"So I can see," Philinna said. "They're not well loved here—people are afraid. Not I, mind, or most of the women, but the men get strange if we remind them. They want to forget such things ever existed."

"Even the king?"

"The king as much as any. Strong women excite him, and he honors the Great Mother for the Power she is. Witchcraft and old goddesses make his privates shrivel."

Myrtale gaped, then laughed.

Philinna grinned. "They really do. His father put Herakles here and moved the Mother into the shadows. Philip won't cast Her out—he's not that set against Her—but he's not Her dearest friend."

"I don't think I am, either," Myrtale said reflectively.

"Then you'll please him well," said Philinna. She stepped carefully past the snakes, with a look that told Myrtale she was not fond of them. "Come, there's much more to see. We won't get into the men's rooms, but the king's hall is always diverting, and the stables—"

"Those I've seen," Myrtale said. "I'd like to stay here for a while, if you don't mind. You don't have to stay. You want to ride in your chariot, yes? I'll go with you another day. Today, I need to pray."

It seemed Philinna understood prayer, if not the need for solitude. She frowned, but she left Myrtale there, surrounded by serpents, with the Mother's image looming over her.

Eighteen

Myrtale prayed for a little while. If the Mother heard, She was silent. Myrtale did not ask Her for anything. She knew what Myrtale needed, as well as what she wanted.

When Philinna was long gone, Myrtale left the shrine. Instead of returning to the women's quarters, she turned in the opposite direction, drawing her veil over her head and walking with a bent and humble posture that made men's eyes slide over her as if she were invisible.

Her hatchling rode with her, asleep in the fold of her chiton. Its small cold presence was remarkably comforting.

This part of the palace was full of men of all stations, voices calling and feet running and an air of bustle and excitement. Next to the quiet of the women's quarters, it was dizzying, but invigorating, too.

They were getting ready for a hunt. The king had had word of a boar that was vexing a village on the plain. For all the buzz and commotion, there was no confusion. Every man knew his place.

Philip was the center around which they spun. The power

of his presence bound them all; when he spoke, they could not help but listen.

Here in the world of men, away from women and Mysteries, he was his purest self. He had an ease about him that she had not seen before, and a strong grace of which she had seen but a shadow. His smile was swift, his gestures expansive; when he laughed, it was a light, free sound.

That side of Philip would never show itself to any woman, no matter how much he loved her. The thought grieved Myrtale more than she might have expected. She wanted all of him—not only the fragment he was willing to give her.

Well, and did she give him all of herself, either? What he saw, she liked to think, was her best face. The sharp edge of her temper, the petty jealousies, and the parts of herself of which she was least proud, she kept hidden from him.

Her aunt would say that this was always so. The woman gave her man her best; in return he gave her his worst.

Myrtale's aunt had even more to say in memory that she had in the living presence. Myrtale shut the door on her firmly and watched the crowd of men and dogs and horses stream out of the palace. From its broad open portico her eyes could follow them far down onto the plain.

She leaned against a column and turned her face to the wind, drinking deep. Part of her would have liked to be out riding with the hunters, but most was pleased to stand here in comfort and watch them dwindle into the distance.

"You could fly with them, you know," Erynna said behind her.

Myrtale neither started nor turned. "I could? Wasn't that one of the lessons you avoided teaching?"

"Destiny intervened," said Erynna. "Are you sorry you're here instead of in Epiros?"

"Another day wouldn't have stretched the thread too thin," Myrtale said.

"I don't control every turn of fate," Erynna said. "I'm here to teach, if you're minded to learn."

"How? When? Here?"

Myrtale heard the laughter in the witch's voice. "Anywhere you like, your majesty."

"I'm not queen yet," said Myrtale, "only the king's most recent acquisition."

"You will be," Erynna said.

Then finally Myrtale turned. The girl was the same as ever: bright-eyed, wicked, crackling with magic. If she had ever regretted anything in her life, Myrtale was not aware of it.

And after all, had it really been a betrayal? Myrtale had won the fight; her uncle had sent her to Philip. She was where she had wanted to be. Now she could have the rest of it—all of it.

She still did not trust Erynna. But to learn to fly—and to learn the rest of the arts she had been eager to learn—she would pay whatever price the witch exacted.

The first part of the lesson was altogether unexpected. Erynna led Myrtale to the room at the farthest end of the women's corridor. It was larger than the others: twice the size, and its walls were crowded with images that though fresh and newly painted seemed as old as the world.

Myrtale had never seen their like—or expected to find Philinna waiting, with plump Phila and a handful of noble-women. It was Philinna who told her where those stiff, angular figures had their origin, painted in flat hues of red and yellow and green, blue and terracotta, white and black. "Egypt," she said, as Myrtale stared at men with beasts' heads and women with elaborately plaited hair and headdresses of tall plumes and trailing ribbons of gold.

"All magic comes from Egypt," Erynna said with a touch of the scholar's chant. "In this place, under the eyes of the gods who brought magic to mortals, we learn the ways that were old before our tribes and nations were born."

The Mother was older, Myrtale thought, nor had She spoken first in Egypt. But mortals had heard Her there, and some of them had gone in time to Dodona. Myrtale was their descendant.

So this was how they had seen the world. While Erynna's half-chant went on, Myrtale circled the room, taking in the images that marched across the walls. One in particular drew her eye: a woman, slender yet richly curved, wearing a headdress that was a coiled snake. There was a flower in her hand.

"That one is a queen," Erynna said.

It was not she who was chanting after all, but Philinna, reading from a book with paintings in it like those on the walls. Myrtale would want to know what words she sang— later. For the moment these images, as large as life, mattered more.

Myrtale's hand brushed the queen's diadem. "Did I know her?" she asked.

For some it might have been a strange, even incomprehensible question. Erynna answered coolly, "You might have long ago. In another life."

"Most would say this is the only life we have."

"Would they?"

"Or maybe I was that queen," Myrtale said. The flicker of Erynna's eyes sharpened her own. "I was, wasn't I? Long ago. Who is this beside her? Is it a ram or a man?"

"That is Amon," Erynna said: "a great god in Egypt."

"Still?"

"Still and always," said Erynna.

Myrtale looked closely at the man with his broad shoulders and narrow flanks and his ram's head—more comely somehow than a bull's, with the curl of its horns matching the curls of its fleece. In their way they made her think of Philip: his blunt features, his thick curling hair.

"Amon," she said. Her voice caressed the name.

"She was his wife," Erynna said: "that queen. She lay with him in sacred rite, and bore him sons who were destined to be kings."

"One son would be enough," Myrtale said. "One sun-bright child. He is the sun, isn't he? I heard that once, long ago. Or maybe in that other life."

"Sun and father," said Erynna, "and king besides."

"So he would be, if his wife were a queen." Myrtale spoke slowly. She felt as if she had wandered into a dream.

Those strange flat figures, twisted to serve a canon that matched nothing in life, took on shape and strength and substance. The queen lowered her eyes and smiled. The god looked on her with a lover's eyes.

His arms were warm and strong. He smelled not of wool or musk as she might have expected, but of flowers: a heavy scent but oddly pleasant, rich and sweet. His lips were a man's; they tasted of honey.

She opened her eyes and stepped back sharply from the wall. Phila was still reading. However strange or deeply real the dream, it had lasted but the space of a breath.

She stared at all these women who desired to learn magic. Did none of them know that magic was not a thing to be ac-

quired? Either it was in them or it was not. They could learn
how to use it—but only if they had it already.

On the edge of dream she could see inside them; she could
see who was like a lamp filled with light, and who was dull
mortal clay. Erynna did not blaze nearly as bright as Myrtale
had expected. Her gift was not to wield magic. It was to
teach—and to make mischief.

The rest were clay—all but Philinna. She was a clear white
flame, with as pure a heart as Myrtale had imagined.

Myrtale was strong, but she had never been pure. She had
too much pride and temper, and too much ambition. She was
Philip's match as none of the others could be.

She met Amon's painted gaze. It was blank, unreadable. It
would come alive when the time came.

She would wait—but not too long. Gods might have infi-
nite patience, but she did not.

"If you want me," she said to him, "best take me while you
can."

He did not answer. He was a god; it would have been beneath him. But she smiled. He had heard her.

PART III

Olympias

Nineteen

Philip got his boar. He came home in a roaring crowd and drank till dawn. None of his wives enjoyed his company that night, nor did he go looking for them.

Myrtale lay alone in her not-quite-wide-enough bed and reflected on a great number of things. In the middle night, a much larger serpentine form joined the hatchling beside her. The Mother's guardian had come to her warmth.

It slept all night in the hollow of her side. In the dark before dawn, she half-woke as it slithered away. She sighed for its absence, before sleep took her again.

The days fell into a rhythm remarkable for two things: magic's presence and Philip's absence. Every day the women gathered among the painted Egyptians to learn spells and cantrips, potions and herb-lore. Every night they slept in their own beds, sometimes together with maids or fellow noblewomen and sometimes alone. Myrtale slept with her hatchling and with the Mother's guardian, night after night.

She had not yet learned to fly. That had been an empty lure—rather like her marriage. Philip had not set foot in the women's quarters since the wedding. He had boys, people said, or rather young men, who kept him entertained when he was not making sons for Macedon.

Myrtale was neither angry nor discouraged. For once in her life, she cultivated patience. She studied her magic and the women around her and the ways of the palace and the voices of men that echoed through the halls. She listened and learned. The matters of war and politics that so fascinated men, to which she had paid little enough attention before, now opened themselves like the books of philosophy and poetry and magic that Philip and his predecessors had gathered like spoils of war.

War was everything here. Macedon was one great army; it was always either mustering or campaigning or preparing for the next campaign. This year, as summer mellowed into autumn, Philip rested as much as he ever could, but that meant endless courts and councils and embassies, and hunts and games and drinking bouts that roared and roistered until morning. Then as if that was not excitement enough, he had his troops out day after day, marching and drilling and fighting mock battles. Once or twice they went out on raids, stayed away for a handful of days, then came back full of boasts and the odd bit of booty.

Philinna and Phila coveted that life. As much as they could, they imitated it with arrows and javelins, footraces and chariot races and hunts of their own that brought back more game than the men's hunts did.

For Myrtale that was no temptation. She turned rather toward the books and the Egyptians' room and the bed that Philip did not choose to visit. Myrtale liked to sit in comfort while the world came to her.

She discovered that if she stayed in one place, kept quiet

and made it clear that she would listen, people would come—sister wives, ladies and servants, even a few of the younger men if she took the afternoon air on the outer portico. They came and offered gifts—a flower, a delicacy, occasionally a jewel—and told her their names and where they came from and why they were in Pella. As she listened—and truly she did listen; she remembered every word, no matter how trivial—they opened to her. They told her things that she suspected they had not told anyone else.

It was an art as mysterious as magic, but there was nothing arcane about it. In those many and varied conversations, she saw patterns of allegiance and loyalty, alliance and hostility. She learned what factions there were in the court, who danced with whom and who would, but for Philip's strong will acting on them all, have been bitter enemies.

The young men were particularly interesting, and the portico was especially pleasant on those long golden days before winter closed in on the mountains. Myrtale took to spending her mornings with books and magic and her afternoons on the portico. The servants had found a chair for her, and her new friends had brought cushions for it, and a table and a service for wine. As the days grew shorter, they vied to bring her warm mantles to shield her against the wind.

Often she saw Philip riding on the plain or heard him speaking in the hall. She listened as best she could, and remembered what she heard; more than once she moved closer, the better to hear it.

She never went in. That would not be approved of. Nor did he ever come out when she was there, though that would have been a welcome thing. She schooled herself not to mind—and that was harder, the longer she went on.

Philip's young men most surely were not afraid of her. Each day there were more of them. She exerted herself to be charming, with arts that were half learned from her sister and half born of instinct. A smile, she knew, could melt a man's heart, and a well-placed word could make him her servant for as long as it pleased her to keep him.

Erynna thought she was a fool. "You have the knowledge and the spells," she said. "You know what to do."

But Myrtale refused. "I won't cast a love spell on any man. If I can't lure and hold him myself, without magic, it's not love, and I don't want it—or him."

"Love *is* a spell," Erynna said, "and he's broken the one you laid on him. Now while you sleep alone, the destiny you came for is slipping away. Unless you take it now, it will be too late."

Myrtale felt a pang at that, a quiver of deep-rooted fear for herself and her choices, but she drove it off with native stubbornness. "I will not trap him with magic."

Erynna retreated, but Myrtale watched her warily. She had a look about her that said she had not given up.

Still, she left off pressing Myrtale, and as far as Myrtale could tell, she raised no powers either for or against Philip. Instead she went back to teaching the royal women and biding her time.

She had tempted Myrtale sorely, but Myrtale stood fast. The more magic she knew, the more securely she could maintain her place here—but not if she had to wield it against the king. There was deep wrongness in that, and no coaxing or cajoling from Erynna would shake her.

As autumn drew on toward winter, the sun's warmth faded. One morning Myrtale woke shivering. Rain drummed on the roof. The mountains were shrouded in cloud, but when the clouds lifted, she knew the summits would be white with snow.

That day no one left the palace. The men crowded into their hall with wine and dice and willing women. The royal women had their own hall, but most gathered in the room that by now was wrapped in a thick mantle of magic.

It was so thick that the room seemed full of smoke. The lamps were lit as always, and Erynna was brewing a concoction of herbs over which she murmured words of power. It was meant, she said, to warm the spirit and make men brave in battle—a fine thing on this cold and cheerless day.

Myrtale found the smell cloying and the air too heavy to breathe. She took refuge in the women's hall, where a lone servant wielded a desultory broom. Phila, who would have nothing to do with magic, was not there; she was still in bed, the servant said.

She was with child, rumor said, though she had not admitted to it. She often kept to herself of late. Myrtale wondered if all was not well; or maybe she simply did not carry easily.

That was not Myrtale's trouble—as little as she liked to acknowledge it. For all the fire of their wedding celebration, in due time her courses had come to mock her. And Philip had not returned to her bed.

It was time to let go of patience. She stirred up the coals in the brazier that stood on its pedestal in the hall's center, spreading her hands over the radiating warmth. There were shapes in the embers, visions both true and false. She rested her eyes on them idly, asking nothing and expecting nothing.

That was dangerous, but she was not afraid. She saw armies marching, bristling with long spears, the *sarissai* of Macedon.

She saw Philip in a plain bronze helmet, then Philip again with his brows bound by a diadem. She saw a city burning—a lovely city of white columns and burgeoning gardens—and a chariot racing on a long course, running far ahead of its rivals.

The embers flared. The sun in splendor, the royal banner of Macedon, rippled in the wind over a golden helmet.

That was not Philip, though he had Philip's foursquare build and slightly bowed legs, and the face had a hint of him: the full cheeks, the firmly rounded jaw. The hair beneath the helmet was ruddy gold; the eyes were grey-green, with such a light in them that Myrtale caught her breath. Either he was divine or he was mad, but he was not a simple mortal man.

He turned as if he had felt her eyes on him, and met her stare. A shiver ran down her spine. It was a pleasurable thrill, but it shook her more than a little.

This one was stronger than she, both for will and power. She had never met anyone of whom she could say as much. Even Philip was her match but not her superior.

The vision dissipated as the embers burst into flame. Myrtale straightened. Her eyes were full of light.

She called for a bath. She demanded perfumes and the finest chiton she had and the jewels she had worn at her wedding. She armed as if for battle, taking her time about it, while the rain drummed down and the wine went round the hall.

Philip hated the rain. It made all the scars ache—damn the things; he was still young, but when the rain kept everyone indoors, he creaked like an old man. The only thing that helped then was a salve he had had from an old witch in Thessaly, worked into the scars by strong young fingers.

He had had to preside in the hall for longer than he liked.

He might have had to stay all day and most of the night if he had not managed to distract the horde of guests and petition-ers with a troupe of actors from Corinth. Under cover of a roaring chorus from the *Bacchae*, he slipped away to the room where Demetrios and the pot of salve were waiting.

It was not Demetrios sitting naked on the bed with the pot in his hands. *She* was there, decorously dressed and veiled, cradling the clay pot in her lap.

From the moment he saw her in the crowd at the Mysteries, her face had haunted his every dream. Asleep and awake, he could think of little apart from her.

He had fought the spell to a standstill. It had compelled him to send Lagos for her—but after all he needed Epiros; he needed every ally he could muster, and marriages were a simple way to ensure them. The rest of his wives had brought him rich dowries, too, and kings bound to fight with him rather than against him. One had already given him a son, a fine and prom-ising image of himself, who if the gods were kind, would be king when Philip had had enough of it.

Those were mortal women. This was something different. The mask of the Mother had not concealed her in the Mys-teries, any more than the Bull's face had concealed his. They had known one another.

She was—not his enemy. He would not call her that. But she was dangerous. She threatened the focus he needed badly, to stay on the throne and keep Macedon strong.

She was already under his skin. If he let himself think of her as anything but the fourth of what he had no doubt would be many royal and politic wives, he would lose his grip. He would care for nothing but her.

Now she was here in his bed, where he had not invited her.

He knew better than to be taken in by that demure posture and those lowered eyelids. There was nothing self-effacing about this child of the Mother.

"What did you do to Demetrios?" he demanded.

It was a rough greeting, but she never flinched. Her voice was low and melodious, a pitch she must have studied as a singer will. It resonated in his bones. "I sent him away," she said.

"It was not your place to do that."

"He is not your wife," she said.

She rose. Though he was braced for whatever she might do, his back stiffened. She was quick, and he well remembered her strength. If she had had a weapon, it would have been at his throat; he could not have stopped her.

Her veil slipped free. So did the pins that confined her hair: by accident or artifice, it tumbled down her back and shoulders to her hips. "Lie down," she said.

He was helpless to disobey her. She was not using witchcraft; he knew the stink of that, and there was none about her, above or below the perfume that made him dizzy. This was her own potent magic, as much a part of her as her clear greygreen eyes.

Her hands were defter than Demetrios' and nearly as strong. They worked the sharply herbal-scented salve into the knots and pits of scars. Philip groaned with pain that melted and flowed into blessed relief.

She had kilted up her chiton to kneel astride him. Her thighs were round and firm, her breasts full and high. They filled his hands.

Her face was as blank as the Mother's mask, but her eyes were burning. They had burned that night, too, when she initiated him into the fullest of the Mysteries—or he initiated her. He too well remembered the moment of resistance, then the blood as he took her maidenhead.

He might have taken that, but he had never taken her. She was not for taking. She would never belong in heart and soul to any man, even the king of Macedon.

He had to take things—men, wives, kingdoms. He was a king. That was what he was for.

He must have spoken aloud, because she answered, "I am your equal. You can't bear that, can you? Everyone is less than you. Except me."

"Only the gods are greater," he said—or gasped. She had slid onto his erect and aching shaft and begun the slow rhythm that was calculated to drive him mad.

When he took a woman or a boy, it was fast, hard, in, out, gone. Not with her. She lingered. She teased. She tormented. Every moment was exquisite and terrifying pleasure.

She kept him just short of climax, holding the moment until his whole body was like to burst. Then with a fierce cry she let him go, tumbling down and clasping him tight and driving him deep. She drained him dry.

He dropped beside her. She drew up her knees and wrapped her arms around herself. "Do you feel it? Do you know what happened?"

Her voice was faint through the ringing in his ears. He had no words to answer.

Her breath gusted warm in his ear. "Never be afraid of this. Never run away from it. We are made for it, you and I. No one else is strong enough, or near enough to gods."

"I'm not afraid," he said. "It's a distraction. I can't afford distractions."

"Nor need you. Are you so simple a man that you can't keep your mind on two things at once?"

"There's a whole world in you."

She raked her nails down his chest, not quite breaking the skin. He grunted at the sharp, small pain and caught her wrist. She stilled. She was smiling. Damn her, was she afraid of nothing?

Foolish question. "Don't ignore me again," she said. "I'll share you—that's the way of the world. But you will be there to be shared."

"Is that an order, madam?"

"If you like," she said, "my king."

She was laughing at him. He hated that. But gods, it made his body burn. He was rising already, impossibly, wanting her all over again.

No one else could do that to him. No one else ever would. He did not know if that was simple knowledge or his heart's promise.

Twenty

It was like taming a wild bull. Philip was large and powerful and deeply dangerous, but more than anything he was afraid. Fear made him run rampant, or else he bolted for far pastures and would not come back.

Myrtale went to him, armed with her will and her smile. He neither drove her from his bed nor sought a bed elsewhere. He faced her on his own ground.

There was not supposed to be a victor or a vanquished. That was hard for him who thought of everything as succeed or fail, win or lose—and if he did not win, it must be a bitter loss. He struggled to see it as a dance of equals.

Very soon, far sooner than any signs might have indicated, Myrtale knew she had conceived. She felt it inside her, only a spark, but so very bright. It burned beneath her heart.

She kept it to herself. Soon enough there would be no hiding it, not among the women who watched and whispered and knew exactly what she did every night. They had wagers with the king's guards as to when her belly would begin to swell. But for this little while, she cherished that most blessed of secrets.

Even Philip did not know. Especially Philip. He might stay away from her then in some Greek folly of protecting the child—as if the love of man and woman could do any harm to the life they had made.

He was less wild now, more willing to accept what was between them, now that he saw it would not shrivel his manhood or keep him from being king. He still had not come to her bed, but his was much more comfortable. She was content with matters as they were.

Not all of it was the body's pleasure, either. He would talk with her afterward, if she encouraged him: telling tales of battles and hunts, during which she struggled to stay awake, but also musing over the plans he had for his kingdom.

"There's so much to do," he said one night, lying on his back with his arms behind his head, staring at the ceiling as if the words of his fate were written there. "So many allies to make, treaties to affirm, wars to win. Enemies to get rid of, too. Athens, now—whatever it can do to stop me, it will. With words alone, if it can."

"That's where all the rumors come from, isn't it?" Myrtale said.

He glanced at her, a quick flash in the lamplight. "That we're all born in barns, and given a choice between a woman and a sheep, we'd tup the sheep?"

"That I know to be false," she said.

He grinned. "What, you won't test it, to be sure?"

"I don't need to," said Myrtale. She sat up and clasped her knees, wrapping herself in blankets for the night was cold. "I should like to learn more of these things. Not war and tactics—those are unbelievably dull—but politics and the ruling of nations. Is there someone who can teach me?"

He did her the courtesy of not laughing at her and asking what a woman would want with such things. "War isn't dull," he said. "War is where it all begins and ends. Tactics in battle extend to the council chamber and the courts of the city or the kingdom."

"Maybe that's what's wrong with them," she said. "They're all backwards."

He seemed torn between laughter and outrage. "You can't have kingdoms without war."

"Not in these days," she granted him. "And yet you all declare that peace is the proper and most desirable state of being. How do you reconcile that? Doesn't it make your head ache?"

"*You* make my head ache," he said.

"Good," she said. "Men don't do enough thinking. They're all at the mercy of their basest impulses."

"And women aren't?"

"We can think of more than one thing at once," she said.

He shook his head. "That's not logic."

"Logic is all the rage in Athens in these days, isn't it? And yet so much of it is false."

"You'll drive me mad," he said, with a growl in it. But he did not order her from his bed.

He did not go to sleep at once, either. He was thinking—of what she had said, she hoped. What he would do with it, she could not be sure, but she trusted that he would put it to good use.

Those were the nights. The days had changed little. No teacher came to instruct Myrtale in the ways of kings and councils.

She did not give away to disappointment—yet. Some things took time.

Although Myrtale had been keeping their husband to herself, her sister wives kept their jealousy in check, if they felt any. Phila might; the others had their children—present or to come—to distract them.

Philinna's son was growing almost visibly. He had learned to run; he ran everywhere, and he talked incessantly, and not infant prattle, either. He asked questions. He wanted to know what things were and how they worked and why. His quick intelligence was a source of delight and frequent consternation to his mother and the servants.

Myrtale was not a woman to take great interest in other women's children. This one was interesting mainly for what it told her about his father—and, maybe, about the child she was carrying. It would be a son, too. She knew that as she knew the rest, because it was the truth.

One cold raw morning, Arrhidaios had escaped his nurse yet again and run naked out of the women's quarters. Myrtale happened to be on the outer portico, wrapped tightly in a mantle, watching the snow fly across the lake and the plain, when he shot past her, laughing.

She caught him without thinking. The force of his speed spun her completely about. When she stopped, she found Erynna staring at her. The rest of the pursuit had veered off toward the men's hall—Erynna's doing, she had no doubt.

"Let him go," the witch said.

"Not unless he can fly," said Myrtale. "He'll pitch right off the cliff."

"Yes," Erynna said.

Arrhidaios was still, warm and heavy in Myrtale's arms. He smelled of milk and clean child. She tucked her mantle around him and stared over his head at Erynna.

"Do think with more than your womb now," Erynna said. "This is the firstborn son. In Macedon that need not mean he inherits, but he will be your son's rival. Two bright stars cannot share this firmament. One of them will destroy the other. Do you want it to be your son who dies?"

Myrtale opened her mouth to deny that she was with child, but that was foolish. Of course the witch knew. Even if she could not see for herself, she could cast a spell or scry in a mirror and discover the truth.

Instead Myrtale said, "I'm capable of many things, but cold-blooded murder, no. My son will be king. This child is no threat to him."

"No?" said Erynna. "True, his mother lacks ambition, but his father more than makes up for it. As, already, does he. He's seduced you as he has everyone else."

Myrtale resisted the urge to spit. "He's a child. It's his nature to seduce grown folk into letting him live. As you say, his mother is not ambitious. She won't put him forward. Nor will his father, once he sees the son I'll give him. This will be a loyal servant and a strong fighting man. He will serve my son. That I know."

"So you fondly imagine," Erynna said. "Cast the bones, lady. Look in the mirror. See what you see."

"I know what I see," said Myrtale. "I see the sun in splendor, and the world bowing before him."

Erynna had an answer for that, too. Myrtale turned away from her, refusing to hear it; she carried the child back to his mother.

Truly Philinna had no ambition. She thanked Myrtale profusely; there were tears. Myrtale escaped before she suffered worse embarrassment.

That night for the first time, Philip came to Myrtale's bed before she went to his. He was lying there when she came in somewhat late and warm with wine—Philinna had insisted on a celebration of her son's return to safety. Myrtale had meant to put on a clean chiton and wash the wine out of her mouth and cleanse it with herbs before she went to her husband, but he had chosen not to wait for her.

She did not need to feign gladness. When he held out his arms, she leaped into them, laughing; and some of that was wine, but most was not.

He was scowling, but she kissed that away, freeing the mirth that she had known was underneath. They were in close quarters there, which she did not mind, but he muttered about bringing in a wider bed. And that was an excellent thing.

She woke from a dream of sunlight and splendor. It was night still; the lamp was burning low. Philip lay motionless beside her, not even breathing.

What she felt was too stark for fear. He was anything but cold in death: it was like lying beside an open fire.

Between them, something moved.

She relaxed and almost laughed. The Mother's snake slid its head along her arm, tasting her scent. "Ah, you missed me," she said softly. "Have I been gone so long?"

Philip went even more still, if that had been possible. When she touched him, he recoiled so violently the bed lurched across the floor. "What—" he tried to say. "What is—"

Myrtale sat up carefully, cradling both snakes in her lap: the hatchling had been coiled at her feet and came up now, drawn by the movement. "These are the Mother's children," she said. "They won't harm you."

He was breathing again—hard; his face was pale. "Gods. You *sleep* with them?"

For so brave a man, he had a remarkable number of fears. Myrtale soothed him as best she could. "They love the warmth."

"I don't love them," he said. His voice was thick.

"They bring the Mother's blessing," she said, "and keep the vermin out, too. Shall I send them away?"

"No."

He did not say it easily, but it was clear he meant it. "They guard you, don't they?" he said. "They let me in. Would they let in anyone else?"

"Not if I didn't wish it."

He nodded. "Good. That's good. Some of the men you've been so friendly with . . . they don't always think with the parts above the waist."

"Maybe not," she said, "but they fear you more than they lust after me."

"I'm nothing to a pair of snakes," Philip said. "You don't mind, I'm sure, if that rumor gets out. They'll say Zeus visits you when I'm not there."

"The only god I have ever shared my bed with, or ever intend to, is the one who lives in you."

He met her eyes. His in that light were dark and deep. "What god is that?"

"What name does it please you to give him? Mother's son, great Amon, Father Zeus—you are all of them, just as I am the Mother. So are all men and women who love one another."

"Not like us," he said.

She smiled. She reached for his hand and laid it on her belly.

His brows rose.

She nodded.

The light in him was so sudden and so bright that she blinked, dazzled. She had expected joy. But this was more.

He had forgotten the Mother's children in the prospect of his own. They dived beneath the blankets as he swept her up and whirled her around the room.

That was a wonder and a delight, but Myrtale had to say it. "It's not your first."

"It will be the best," he said. "Don't tell me you don't feel it."

"From the beginning," she said. "You can. You really can see."

"You're surprised?"

She thought to deny it, but that would not be the truth. "You're so much a man of this world. Even with the Mysteries . . . I didn't think . . ."

"I never do the expected thing," he said.

As in war, so in all else. She nodded slowly. He had given her a gift of sorts.

They came to rest beside the bed. He set her lightly on her feet; she rested against him. He was not a tender man, but he held her for as long as she wished to be held, and that too was a gift.

When she withdrew, he lifted her and laid her in the bed. Then he lay beside her, propped on his elbow, and drank her in.

Both of her. As fleeting as that might be, she basked in it. She had earned it—and so would the son they had made.

The next morning, men brought in a new and larger bed, which nearly filled the room. With it they brought a brazier and a boy to tend it, and a chest full of gifts: chitons and mantles and veils, and a box so heavy it took two men to lift, full of golden ornaments.

A pair of maids came with the rest. No witches these, and no slaves, either; they were free Macedonian women, well trained and apparently well disposed toward the king's wife. They seemed to find it more amusing than not that the king was so besotted.

"He likes you," said the elder of the two sisters. Her name was Phryne; the younger was Baukis. "Mostly, he only likes women to make sons with—even if they wear armor and best him at the hunt. You, he respects."

From a Macedonian, that was high praise. Myrtale let herself bask briefly in it before she took thought for the consequences of Philip's extravagance.

She could not send the gifts or the maids away—that would offend him beyond forgiveness. But she had to live with her sister wives. Even Philinna might not take kindly to the favor shown Myrtale, when she had borne her husband a son to much less fanfare.

But if Myrtale divided the gifts, she would seem either ungrateful or arrogant. Philip had left her with a dilemma—damn him.

She would carry on as always. No apologies. In this world, one ruled or one served. Generosity was a virtue, but first one had to have the gifts to give. And for that, one had to rule.

This morning, at last, Erynna professed herself willing to teach her pupils to fly. They were all there but Philinna—she had a winter rheum, Audata said. That was unfortunate: she had been the most eager of them all. But no one was minded to wait for her.

The secret proved rather disappointing. It was an ointment made of olive oil and sheep's fat and a mixture of herbs. The art was in the mixing, and in the words one spoke as one did it—and, Myrtale could see, the power one brought to the work.

Erynna had a small quantity of all but one of the herbs; that one, she declared, had to be gathered with a golden sickle by the first light of the new moon. Without it, the rest was no more than a vaguely astringent, rather unpleasantly numbing salve.

"In the spring," Erynna promised, "when the earth comes to life again, we'll finish this. We'll fly against the moon."

She was full of promises, that one. Myrtale packed away her little jar of ointment, useless as it was without its final tincture.

She had been careful to wash her hand where it had tested the mixing, but the numbness lingered. As it was now, it was a rather nasty poison. She had her doubts that, once finished, it would be any less dangerous.

Did the witches really fly, then? Or did they leave their bodies in a fever dream, and only return by the Mother's mercy? How many of them died of it?

Magic did not frighten Myrtale. This made her wary. She thrust the jar deep in her chest of belongings, down at the bottom, and resolved to forget it existed.

Twenty-one

Philip came late to Myrtale's bed that night, but he did come. She woke from a doze to find him warm and heavy against her, snoring softly. She thought of waking him with kisses, but it was pleasant just to lie there beside him and listen to the wind.

It was wailing tonight, promising another storm before morning. Myrtale shifted carefully, so as not to wake Philip.

She was warm and comfortable and safe. And yet she could not stay still. The wind's wailing rose in pitch until she stuffed the blankets into her ears; then it filled her head from within.

It was not the wind. Philip stirred beside her and sat up, blinking and scowling.

Myrtale was already on her feet and wrapped in a mantle. She snatched up the lamp and shielded the flame as she peered out into the corridor.

It was full of shadows: people running toward the outcry. Philip pushed past Myrtale and flung himself into the current. She half ran in his wake.

The wailing came from the women's hall. Philinna crouched there, clutching a bundle to her breast, rocking and keening. Servants struggled with her, trying with varying degrees of gentleness to take the bundle away, but she only clung the tighter.

Myrtale stepped around Philip and knelt beside Philinna. Her eyes were almost completely empty of sense, but as they fixed on Myrtale, slow recognition dawned. Then her clasp loosened enough so that Myrtale could see what she held.

It was her son Arrhidaios. His body was limp; his head lolled. His lips were blue.

He was still warm—with his mother's warmth? Myrtale laid her hand against his cheek.

Life slept deep within him. It was rapidly growing cold. "Philinna," Myrtale said. Then louder: "Philinna!"

Her sister wife stopped rocking and wailing. "He's alive," Myrtale said. "Do you hear me? You have to let him go. If I can help—"

Philinna thrust the child into Myrtale's arms so suddenly that Myrtale nearly dropped him. He was a surprisingly heavy weight, slack and barely breathing. But he was breathing.

She had never studied this kind of magic. It *was* magic and not only poison—she could taste it, thick and bitter on the back of her tongue. She had only what she knew, and what her heart told her.

She sank down to the floor under the weight of so much treachery. When the magic came out of her, it came in a word-less song, a melody such as a mother would sing to lull her child to sleep. It seemed right that she should rock Arrhidaios as she sang, cradling him while the wind howled beyond the walls.

Winter had set in fast and hard. It was sunk in the child's bones.

The life in him burned low. What was a bright flame in the

rest of them was pale and cold in the child. Myrtale fed it with her own fierce heat.

It warmed a little, but it had burned down too far. She could keep it alive, but only just, for all her singing and wishing and, as the magic drained out of her, praying.

She looked up from his lolling head to the ring of staring faces. Some had turned hostile. She felt rather than heard the word they whispered, like a gust of foul air in her face: *Witch.*

That was true, but it was not her witchery that had felled Arrhidaios. Her eyes found the witch in the shadows beyond the crowd. Erynna was smiling.

The sun was out of reach, but the moon rode beyond the clouds. Its borrowed light lacked the strength to do real harm, but a lash of it could sting.

Erynna went down, convulsed. Myrtale put her out of mind. "Philinna," she said. "Take him. Keep him warm and pray. I've done all I can do."

"That's more than enough," someone muttered. Myrtale could not see who it was.

It was not one of her sister wives, and it was not Philip. They were all who mattered. Myrtale returned the child to his mother, who had come to herself somewhat, and rose stiffly.

She felt cold and ill, and her bones ached. The working she had done, for as little good as it did, had drained her. That was Erynna's darker magic, sapping all else of strength—and Arrhidaios most of all.

"Will he live?"

Myrtale stared without recognition. Slowly it dawned on her that the man who spoke was her husband. Equally slowly, she mustered a response. "That is with the Mother."

He swayed; his face blurred. Myrtale reached, perhaps to

steady him, perhaps to catch herself. His hands were strong and familiar. She let them hold her up.

Everything was floating, and it all seemed very far away. She had never felt quite like this before. There was more to it than magic. Was she ill?

The one clear thing in this world of mist and shadow was fear. The child within her, hardly more than a spark—if he died because of this—

The Mother's arms closed about her, even warmer and stronger than Philip's. Myrtale clung to the fear, but it slid away in spite of her, melting between her fingers. When all of it was gone, there was sleep, sweet and deep.

For nine days Arrhidaios lay between life and death. His mother and his nurses kept him warm and massaged his limbs and fed him sops of milk and honey. His father sacrificed a new lamb to Hera and a white bull to Father Zeus, for such good as they might do.

To the Mother Philip would give nothing. "This is Her doing," he said to Myrtale.

He was still coming to her bed—which surprised her somewhat. But his anger did not seem to have extended itself to her; he was one of the few of whom that could be said.

On that night, the ninth night, he paced the room, even as small as it was. His shoulders were hunched; his shadow leaped toward the ceiling as the wind of his passage made the lamp's flame burn tall. His voice was a growl. "She did this," he said. "She hates me because I won't crawl at Her feet. My gods are younger gods, stronger gods. Gods who wield greater power in this age of the world."

"No one is stronger than the Mother," Myrtale said, "and She had nothing to do with this. This is witchcraft, plain and mortally simple."

"I don't believe in witches," Philip said. His voice was flat.

"You should," said Myrtale. "I saw the witch gloating over her handiwork."

"They say you did it," he said. "You poisoned him to protect your own interest."

Her heart went still, but her eyes held steady. "Do you believe that?"

"I believe you would do anything to get what you want. But this? It's too petty. You'd kill him outright, and get rid of his mother, too."

"I wouldn't trouble," Myrtale said. "She has no ambition. He might, if he grows up—but I think he'll make a better servant than king."

"A king needs good servants," Philip said. He reached for her in sudden hunger—no Greek nonsense after all; his child in her made him want her more than ever. But before he took her, he paused. "Who is it? Who's the witch?"

"Where do witches come from?"

He pulled back, scowling. "You'd mock me with riddles now?"

"You sent me a servant," she said, "but since you don't believe in witches, I suppose it didn't occur to you that a woman from Thessaly might be more than a bold-eyed maid."

His back stiffened. "I'll kill her. I'll throttle her with my own hands."

"Don't," said Myrtale. "Leave her to me."

"No," Philip said. "Not this one."

"Yes," she said. It was hard: he had power in his presence, and it pressed on her. But she was stronger than he. She stared him down.

He disliked that intensely, but it excited him, too. He pulled her to him, hard, and made a show of taking her by storm.

Even in grief and anger, he could make her smile. But she had not forgotten a word they had said.

Myrtale bided her time. If Erynna had expected to be caught, each day's passing would have lulled her further into complacence.

On the day after Myrtale spoke to Philip, Arrhidaios began to wake. It was slow; he was weak. He seemed to recognize no one, not even his mother.

It was as if he had returned to infancy and must begin all over. All his bright quickness was gone. He was alive, and he seemed content—if nothing else, he could smile, and he seemed to take pleasure in such life as he had—but he was a broken thing. Neither medicine nor magic could mend him.

His father sent for physicians from Athens and Corinth. His mother called on every herb-healer and hedge-witch and diviner who could be found in the dead of winter. She even sent messengers to Persia to find someone, anyone, who might heal her child.

Philinna had hope. Myrtale almost envied her. The truth was a bitter draught.

No one said anything, but the lessons in the room of the Egyptians had stopped. The door was shut and no one passed it. The little bits of songs and spells that had followed the witch's pupils about the palace were silenced; the potions were poured out and the herbs scattered on the wind. It was a repudiation in every way, but done in silence, with no words exchanged.

Erynna seemed to have vanished, but Myrtale could still smell her. She was somewhere in Pella.

Myrtale hoped the witch was living in dread of the king, but that was as unlikely as Arrhidaios' return to the child he had been. Erynna was not done. Whatever she was plotting, there was more to come.

Carefully and with utmost discretion, as winter warmed once more into spring, Myrtale wove protections for herself and her husband, and upon reflection, for her sister wives, too.

This was not the witchcraft of Thessaly. It was older and stronger. She drew it up from deep within herself, shaping it out of the earth, from the Mother's bones.

She had not known she could do such a thing until she did it. When she reflected on the need to guard what she cherished, the answer was there, filling her hands like a flood of sunlight.

There was more to magic than words and potions. Words limited it. Potions barely began to draw upon the fullness of power.

Myrtale knew all too well how dangerous raw power could be. But she was not the ignorant girl who had pulled the sun out of the sky. She had some small understanding now, and some sense of restraint.

And she had the child growing inside her. What Erynna had done to Arrhidaios, she would never do to Myrtale's son.

Myrtale swore that as an oath before the Mother, sealed with blood and magic. Myrtale's son would live and grow and thrive. No evil thing would touch him.

She made that great prayer in the shrine by the palace gate, on yet another night of storm in a long and brutal winter. Philip was still in the hall, roaring through one of the long drinking bouts that had grown more numerous as the dark days passed. Faint echoes of it reverberated among the pillars.

Myrtale stood before the image of the Mother. Her swelling belly felt heavy; her back ached. And yet that ache was a wonderful thing, because there was life inside, and it was drumming insistently on the walls of its world.

For him she prayed, putting all her heart in it, with her soul and everything else she had. She left it to the Mother to choose what protections She would raise, but Myrtale left no doubt that they would be there and they would be strong.

It was monstrously presumptuous. Myrtale did not care. This was her child. He needed his father; he needed his kin. Yes, even his stepmothers, who were part of the kingdom that his father would pass to him when he was grown.

"Protect them," Myrtale beseeched the Mother. "Guard them. Preserve them from harm."

Twenty-two

"Pity you left that prayer so late."

Myrtale whipped about. The voice was so unexpected and the speaker so completely unlooked for that for a moment she did not recognize the woman at all.

Then the world sharpened into focus. Her aunt stood in the center of the hall, mantled in black as always, looking not a day older or a fraction less forbidding than she had when last Myrtale saw her.

It was startling to realize that her aunt was young—or at least not old. She had been so terrible a presence for so long, but here in this alien place, she had shrunk to mortal stature and rather less than august age. She was not so very much older than Philip.

Myrtale was in no way minded to underestimate her. She stood calmly in the light of the lamps, showing no sign of either rage or longing for revenge. She must not have been caught in Myrtale's spell for long, then.

That was a relief of sorts, though it was also a warning. If Myrtale ever hoped to do such a thing again, she would have to fight for every step of it.

She let none of that show on her face. "Aunt," she said. "Welcome. What brings you to Macedon?"

"The wind," her aunt answered, "and the Mother's will."

"You flew?" That escaped before Myrtale could stop it. She bit her tongue.

Her aunt did not answer directly. She said, "Witchcraft is a shallow mockery of true magic."

"I had come to that conclusion myself," Myrtale said.

"Had you?" Her aunt turned slowly, taking in the broad circle of the shrine. "So. They remember Her here, even yet."

"This is still Her country," Myrtale said.

"So it seems." Her aunt approached the Mother's image, bowed and murmured a prayer.

Myrtale resisted the urge to retreat. Whatever her aunt meant to do here, Myrtale would be safe. She had bound the Mother to that.

Her aunt straightened and turned. "Well, child. Will you make me welcome?"

Myrtale would rather not. But hospitality was sacred; she would do herself more harm by refusing it than by offering it, even to this of all people.

Strangely, she felt no danger in this woman. Her aunt seemed somehow to belong here, as if she had been meant to come to this place. If she had come to take revenge, there was no reek of it about her.

That gave Myrtale pause. She pondered it while she called servants and arranged lodging and saw her unexpected guest fed and given the best wine to drink. Her aunt conducted herself properly, with respect and thanks, which only made Myrtale the more wary.

She of all women was not here out of the goodness of her heart. If she had any concern for her niece, it was more likely fear of what havoc Myrtale might wreak upon this country she had chosen.

Not so long ago, that concern would have been well founded. But that was before Myrtale woke to herself— before life woke in her and changed the way she saw the world.

She was still dangerous; more so than ever. She was stronger and surer and more skilled. And she had her child to protect. Nothing mattered more than that.

Myrtale had more than half expected her aunt to appear in her bedchamber before morning, but neither the priestess nor her husband came to trouble her rest. Her aunt's absence was a relief. Philip's needed thinking on—tomorrow.

Tonight there were dreams. These were not heedless ivory dreams, wishes and hopes and airy fancies. They came through the gate of horn, deceptively plain and unadorned, as the truth should be.

Even in the midst of each dream, Myrtale felt the power that dwelt in all of them. They rose out of the earth beneath her and the magic in her.

She stood on the shore of the sea. The white strand stretched away before her. Black cliffs rose above her. The air was sharp and clean; the sky was fiercely, bitterly blue.

Some little distance from the shore, a rock thrust out of the waves. A woman sat there, trailing long white fingers in the water. Her hair streamed down her back, as white as foam, with a faint but distinct green tinge.

Her chiton seemed woven of sea-wrack and spume, held to-gether with glimmering shells. But that barely caught Myrtale's eye. Of much more interest was the shape of her beneath the odd garment.

She was swollen with child as Myrtale was, and there was such a light on her as Myrtale knew well. There was splendor growing inside her.

Even in dream, Myrtale felt the prickle of small hairs on her nape. She knew who this had to be—and if it was, then this was a world long ago, a thousand years gone.

The sea-nymph raised her head. She was as beautiful as a goddess should be, even a minor goddess. The Mother was in her, much clearer and closer than She ever could be in mortal flesh.

Her eyes were as changeable as the sea. They stared straight into Myrtale's own. "They make the choice," she said, "but we bear the brunt."

Myrtale frowned. Gods could be elliptical, and their minds did not run on simple tracks as mortals' did, but this was more oblique than most.

Before she could ask what the goddess meant, the sea rose and overwhelmed the world. When it subsided, the strand and the headland were gone. Myrtale looked out across a windy plain to a city of innumerable towers.

The sea was calmer here, the strand longer—much longer. Ships were drawn up on it, and a city of tents rose between the city of stone and the sea. Light glinted on helmet and spearpoint.

The goddess spoke beside Myrtale. "Give a man a choice, and war is what he chooses. Forbid him choice, and he goes to war to win it."

"Can a man be a hero without war?" Myrtale inquired.

"In the old time he could," said the goddess. "Someday maybe again. But now . . ."

"I don't want to change the world," Myrtale said. "I want to rule it. I want my son to rule it."

"Sons will do what they will do," the goddess said.

"Mine will rule," said Myrtale. Her hand had come to rest over her belly, where he danced his war-dance beneath the arch of her ribs.

"I kept my son too close," the goddess said, "and yet not close enough. Be wary of that. The balance is delicate and the dangers great; one false step and he is lost forever."

"I won't lose him," Myrtale said fiercely through the shiver of fear in her gut, "and I won't lose my husband, either."

"Can you help it? They want complaisant women, soft and helpless. Strength is no virtue in these days."

Myrtale looked directly into those shimmering eyes. It struck her with a shock: she was no weaker than this goddess, though her flesh was mortal. As for what she carried in her . . .

They were the same. This child of glory who had grown into the great Achilles was the same heart and spirit that rode in Myrtale now. He had come back.

The goddess inclined her head. "May you and yours fare better than we."

There was something terrifying about that simple and stately courtesy. Achilles had had a choice, which the gods had given him through his mother: a long and unsung life and a quiet death, or one brief flash of brilliance and then, for him, oblivion—but for his name, life everlasting.

In Egypt the name was everything. As long as it lived in memory, so did the soul. If it was erased or forgotten, the soul was gone, vanished into nothingness.

"I'll make the choice," Myrtale said. "I won't subject him to it. If I can choose—"

"You may not," the goddess said.

"Why? I'm his mother. That gives me the right—"

"Not for this one," said the goddess.

She swept her hand over the plain, which had shrunk to the size of Myrtale's coverlet. Mist rose, then cleared.

The tents were not so different. There was a sea and a shore, and in the distance a city. But the spears were the long spears of Macedon, and the faces were Macedonian faces.

There was one in a golden helmet, a flame that leaped up to heaven. Myrtale peered closer. Her back was taut with eagerness.

The mist thickened. The coverlet rippled. The vision melted away before the grey light of dawn and the cold smell of grief.

Myrtale lay still, half in dream and half awake. Strange, she thought, that she had not dreamed of Philinna's child or the witch who had poisoned him.

That was true and present and incontestable. The rest was dream and promise.

She turned her head and saw without surprise that Erynna sat in the corner, watching her. It was so very simple to find the fire inside and arm it and gather herself to smite.

Then Erynna said, "I did it for you."

The flare of magic collapsed upon itself. Myrtale lay cold and empty and—not afraid, no. But not in comfort, either.

She had anger enough to keep her warm, if she could reach it. "You did nothing for me. I would never countenance—"

"That," said Erynna, "was your son's most bitter rival."

"He was no threat to my child," Myrtale said.

"Nor shall he be." Erynna tucked up her feet. She was floating in air, shimmering faintly.

Myrtale's nose twitched. Was that the pungent scent of the witches' ointment? Or was she imagining it? "Get out," Myrtale said.

The witch tilted her head. Her eyes were glittering, but the smile lingered on her lips. "I don't think so," she said.

Myrtale sat up. She was both remarkably calm and remarkably angry. "Leave now," she said, "or I'll have you carried out."

"You may do that," said Erynna, "but you may regret it."

She had no fear at all. Nor did Myrtale, but her estimation of this witch had shifted upward. There was little enough power there—that had not been a deception—but the bait did not need more. Those who wielded her, however . . .

If Myrtale gave way to her, that would only be the beginning. Or had it all begun long ago? Was she bound to the witches in some way she could not understand?

When she opened her mouth to speak, the words came freely enough. No bolt of divine wrath struck her, nor did a poisonous spell close her throat. "Out," she said. "Go."

Erynna shrugged. "As you will," she said.

Twenty-three

The witch had surrendered too easily, but Myrtale took such advantage from it as she could. As soon as Erynna was gone, Myrtale sought out her maids on their pallets by the wall and tried to shake them awake. They did not stir: they were drugged, and not subtly, either.

Myrtale had to bow to Erynna's cleverness. If magic had cast them into sleep, Myrtale would have sensed it. A plain and ordinary sleeping draught had eluded her notice.

After a long while and a dash of cold water to the face, Baukis roused to a mumbling half-stupor. Phryne was breathing, but there was no waking her.

Myrtale gave up any hope of rousing them before morning. She left them where they lay, snatched up her warmest mantle and ventured out into the corridor.

All the lamps had burned down, but she knew her way in the dark. The one she looked for was such a light of magic as was seldom seen in this place.

. . .

Her aunt was awake, sitting upright by lamplight, waiting. Myrtale resisted the urge to duck her head and mime submission. Old habit was strong, but she was stronger.

She straightened her back and met that level stare. "I think," she said, "it's time you told me all the things you've been keeping from me."

"Why should I do that?" her aunt asked. "You've done well enough without them."

"That was luck and the Mother's hand," said Myrtale. "If you won't talk, I'll send to Epiros and drag back the other priestesses. Snow in the mountain passes didn't stop you. It won't stop them, either."

"The Promeneia you knew is dead. There is only one priestess still in Dodona."

That brought Myrtale up short. She rallied her wits as quickly as she could. "Then you are—"

"Timarete," her aunt said.

Myrtale spared an instant's grief for the eldest priestess, who had always been kind to her. But there was no time to indulge in it. "You're here because of the witch, aren't you? What took you so long?"

"A certain spell," Timarete answered dryly, "and a much increased burden on the temple, now that one of our priestesses is gone."

"Train Attalos," Myrtale said. "He's got the mind for it, and he has enough magic to manage. He can do as much as you need until you find a woman fit to be Nikandra."

Timarete arched a brow. "You care what we do?"

"No," Myrtale said, snapping off the word. "If you've come to drag me back there, you can disabuse yourself of the notion. I won't be forced into it by guilt or grief. This is where I belong. I was never meant for Dodona."

"You were not," said Timarete. Strange to see that name attached to that face, so unlike the gentle woman who had held it before. "Maybe I had hopes. I am human, as difficult as that may be to comprehend. But I haven't come for that."

Myrtale refused to be taken aback. Always expect the unexpected—that was Philip's maxim. "Then why have you come?"

"May I not visit my kinswoman?"

"In the dead of winter? With all that's happened in your temple?" Myrtale clenched her fists at her sides to keep from clamping them around that smooth white throat. "We can dance around the truth until the earth rises and swallows us. Isn't that what you've done since the day I was born?"

Timarete's face had gone still. "Can you say for certain that I was wrong to have done it?"

"Yes!" said Myrtale with sudden heat. "You left me open to *that.*"

"Did I?"

"If I had known what I was," she said—barely able to get the words out; her throat kept trying to close—"I would never have fallen into the witches' trap. I would never have—"

"You don't know that," Timarete said.

Myrtale had done her utmost to face her aunt with a steady heart and a calm mind. But that blank face and those useless words tore to shreds all her noble ambitions. "You blinded and deafened me and made me live with a fraction of the senses I was born with. You taught me nothing, showed me nothing, did nothing. I was ripe for the first hunting beast that came upon me."

If Timarete had asked another of her damnable questions, Myrtale would have killed her. But she was silent, sitting up in the borrowed bed, offering no more with face or glance than she ever had.

Then she said, "The omens of your birth were so black there were those who argued in favor of giving you to the wolves. I fought for you, because you are my own blood and because we needed you in the temple. Did we truly teach you nothing? Did we raise you so badly?"

Myrtale shook off all but the part that mattered. "What were the omens? What did you foresee?"

She held her breath against another prevarication. Timarete startled her with as straight an answer as she could have asked for. "We saw the sun come down and the world end in fire."

"Ah," said Myrtale as the words sank in. "Is that all? You saw my foolishness with the oracle, then. Now it's over. There was somewhat to fear, and a good woman died. But the world is still here; the rest of us are still alive."

"Maybe so," Timarete said, "but I think not. There's worse to come."

"Only if you will it into being."

"You've grown," said her aunt, "and grown almost wise, but you're no less a fool than I ever was. Do you think the Fates will let you be simply because you've decided you'll not play their game?"

"No," Myrtale said, "but I do think a strong enough will and a wise enough heart can persuade them to alter one's destiny."

"Even the gods aren't as wise or as strong as that."

"Maybe," said Myrtale. "Maybe I'll dare to hope."

"After what you've seen, you can say that?"

"Would you rather I flung myself down, wailing in despair?"

Myrtale stood over the bed. She knew she was looming; she hoped it gave Timarete at least a moment's pause. "If I don't hold to hope, I'll have no courage left. Will you help me? I know I have no right to ask it. I do not want my fate to unwind as you've foreseen it."

"No one does," Timarete said.

"Except Erynna," said Myrtale.

Timarete arched a brow. "The witch? She threatened you?"

"In her way," said Myrtale, "she challenged me."

That caught her aunt's attention. "Did she threaten you?"

Myrtale shrugged, but after a moment she judged it wise to answer. "She did imply it."

"Of course she did," Timarete said. "Did she name any names? Speak of anyone else who might be conspiring with her?"

"No," Myrtale said.

"Pity," said Timarete. She rose briskly. "You'll sleep here tonight. And you *will* sleep. You've a child to think of."

"That's what they want," Myrtale said, and shuddered. "They want him. Not to kill him but to rule him—to make him their creature."

"That may be," her aunt said, "but you're no lesser prize, either."

"They only want me for what I can give them. Him they can shape as they please. Since," said Myrtale, "they failed with me."

Timarete's eyes were unreadable. "Come now. Into bed. This room is safe; there's nothing to fear here. But don't pass the door again until morning."

A good part of Myrtale resisted. She was not a child any longer, to be ordered about so. But Timarete was wiser than she, and better trained, too—no matter whose fault that was.

Myrtale curled in the bed that was still warm from her aunt's body, arms circling her middle, guarding the life that grew there. The walls enclosed a singing silence. Even the howl of the wind was faint and far away.

For once in her life, Timarete's niece was choosing to be obedient. Timarete wondered if she should be suspicious. Probably; but she had more pressing concerns.

She laid words of guard on the door, strong enough that they left her dizzy and stumbling, but she found her feet again soon enough. She passed through the palace like a shadow and a shimmer, searching for the stench of the darker magics.

She found her fair share of those, but the youngest was a day and more old. More than one power had cast them, but they all had a scent of the witch whom she knew.

Erynna was not in the palace. If she was still in Pella, she had hidden herself well. That was no more than Myrtale had found, but Timarete looked farther and deeper than her niece had been able to.

By the time Timarete made her way back to the room in which she had left Myrtale, the palace was warded from top to bottom. A powerful blast of magic could still pierce those walls, but anything less would rebound like an arrow from a fortress wall.

She was lightheaded with exhaustion. That was a dangerous state to be in, but it was also a peculiarly magical one. If she could keep a grip on what strength and skill she had left, she might succeed in learning something she had not known before.

It was profoundly tempting to take that magic, find the enemy and wield it against her. But Timarete's heart was uneasy.

She had to be sure that Myrtale was safe—that nothing that could do her harm had hidden itself inside the wards.

Timarete could appreciate the irony of that. Time was when she would have been glad to have this troublesome child taken off her hands. But the call of blood was strong. She did not want to destroy the girl; only to keep her from destroying everyone else.

Myrtale was asleep, drawn into a knot under the coverlets of silk and fur. She had guardians: the largest house-snake Timarete had ever seen raised its head from beside Myrtale's, eyes glittering in the lamplight. A second, much smaller and darker shape coiled against the girl's back.

Timarete bowed to the Mother's children. Nothing would touch Myrtale while they watched over her.

She stayed there nonetheless, sitting close by the brazier, drinking in its warmth. Visions woke in the coals, a world of shimmering fire that dissolved into chill reality.

Twenty-four

Winter broke with supernatural suddenness. One evening the cold rain fled before a colder blast of wind. The next morning the crack of cold gave way to a lingering warmth. By afternoon even the old folk who had shivered all winter beside the fire had put aside their swathings of wool and fur and hobbled out to bask in the sun.

Myrtale emerged with them, standing on the portico above the black and tumbled waters of the lake and letting the wind blow the darkness out of her spirit. No one came near her; at first she barely noticed, but as the wind died down and the warmth rose, she realized that everyone who had been coming and going down or through the portico had walked wide of her.

Her days of seclusion had done nothing to soften their hostility. *Witch,* they called her, not even trying to hide the signs and gestures against the evil eye. Whatever Erynna had done, they ascribed to Myrtale, and they hated her for it.

She stayed where she was, defiant at first, and then determined. They would come to see who had laid this curse on them, after Myrtale had dealt with it.

The child, who had been quiet within, stirred and kicked hard. She caught her breath and pressed her hand to her middle. For a long moment she floated with him in a warm, dim sea. The power that would fill him was not even a spark as yet, only a dream and a promise.

When she opened her eyes to the mortal world again, the sun was notably closer to the western horizon than it had been. The men she had seen departing from the palace were loping back in, flushed and filthy and full of their own splendor. Whatever they had been doing—running or fighting or racing with chariots—had pleased them well.

Those who caught her gaze on them turned away sharply; one or two even drew up a fold of mantle. Myrtale had vowed to herself that she would not give way to temper, but she had reached the edge of endurance.

She set herself in front of one who had tried to hide behind his cloak. He was a man of middle age, with grey in his beard and a look about him that spoke of a long sense of grievance with the world. Myrtale had seen him in the hall, sitting midway down the ranks of nobles, neither the highest nor the lowest of them.

Clearly he felt he should have sat higher, and that rankled in him. It was all too easy for such a man to look for blame to cast, and easier yet if he could blame a woman.

Myrtale bestowed on him her most brilliant smile. "Good evening, my lord Kleitos. Would you be so kind as to escort me to my rooms?" As she spoke, she swayed slightly, as if to belie the smile's bravado with womanly weakness.

She felt his shudder in her own skin, but he had been well and ruthlessly trained. However he might loathe her, she was the king's wife. With eyes flat and lips a thin line, he bowed stiffly and tilted his chin toward the door.

He was not going to gratify her with a word or a glance. She pretended not to notice. When she leaned on his arm, he went even more rigid than before, but he stopped short of flinging her off. She leaned more heavily, until he was almost carrying her. "Truly the gods have sent you to my aid," she said, taking several breaths to do it.

People were watching. Her reluctant protector must have been outspoken about the witch from Epiros: eyes widened, heads shook. Men muttered to one another, but she could not both play her game and catch the words.

Their expressions were clear enough, and their eyes flicking from the manifest beauty of her face to the king's child growing beneath her girdle. It was harder to hold to fear and hate when the object of both was female and young. That she was also royal and beautiful confounded them utterly.

She wanted that confusion, if it forced them to think past the curse to the truth. When Kleitos left her at the door to the women's quarters, his relief was palpable, but the worst of his loathing had passed. She thanked him as prettily as she knew how, and left him as gratefully as, she had no doubt, he left her.

She shut the door and leaned on it. This time her weakness was not feigned. She had spent a great deal of strength in that working.

It was worth the price. The greyness in the air was perceptibly less. The hatred that battered against her defenses was slightly less potent.

After a few dozen breaths, she was able to stand again and

walk. She had not been thinking on anything past the men and their follies, but her mind had made itself up.

Timarete was nowhere to be found. Myrtale quelled the quick anger: if her aunt had gone back to Epiros, she would have known it. Either Timarete was away because she chose to be, or—

Myrtale would have known if she had been abducted, too. The web of power within the palace would have screamed with it.

As she thought of that, she searched through the interwoven strands of magic both good and ill, and the spirits of the human creatures who lived within it. Then at last she found Timarete, well away from the women's quarters, deep among the men, still and quiet behind the hall.

It was harder to find her in the flesh than in the spirit. Most of the men had gone in to dinner, but the corridors were full of slaves and servants. Their constant movement and chatter rattled Myrtale's skull.

She nearly lost the skein of Timarete's magic, and had to struggle to keep her grip on it, stumbling and groping along the wall. None of the servants spared her a glance. She detected no malice there, but no interest, either.

That suited her admirably. She paused to gather her wits. Men's voices in the hall were growing louder: the wine had begun to go round.

Thinking of wine made her dizzy. She was too far down in the magic, but she dared not rise higher, lest she lose the quarry. She walked slowly, picking her way as if blind.

The babble of voices faded from her awareness. All that was left was a sense, as near as her skin, of Philip's strong fierce presence. He was not the one she hunted, but it comforted her to know where he was.

The hunt ended much more swiftly than she had expected. She found herself in front of what at first seemed a blank wall, until she saw the outline of a door. It was cleverly hidden, but it was not locked or barred: it opened easily to her touch.

The room beyond was small but well appointed, furnished with a couch in the Persian style, a wine-table, a carved wooden chair, and a common stool such as one might find in any poor man's house. Timarete perched on the stool with her back to the door and her ear to the wall.

As Myrtale approached, she saw that what she had taken for a shadow on the wall was the grating of a window that looked down into the hall. The view was remarkably extensive, and so was the clarity of sound that rose up from below.

She turned toward Timarete, brow lifted. Timarete answered the unspoken question in the breath of a whisper. "Every king has a spyhole; he's a fool if he doesn't. Didn't you know?"

"There's much I don't know," Myrtale said more softly still. "Have you learned anything useful?"

"Not today," said Timarete, rising from the stool and shaking out her skirts.

She left the room so quickly that she caught Myrtale flat-footed. She did not pause to let Myrtale catch her, either, but strode down the passage as she did everywhere, with head up and back straight.

In the Mother's shrine, at last, she stopped. The men's gods loomed in the dimness, but Timarete paid no heed to them.

She bowed to the Mother, showing every sign of intending to spend the night in prayer.

Myrtale set herself between Timarete and the Mother's image. "There's not much time left," she said.

"There is not," said Timarete. "Are you ready?"

"Does it matter?"

"No," said Timarete.

Myrtale nodded. Then: "What did you hear?"

"Nothing that matters to us," Timarete said, "but you might get some use of the place where you found me, after this is done—if you choose."

"You would have me spy on my husband?"

"Is it spying if he knows?"

"He knows you were there?"

Timarete shrugged slightly. "It wouldn't surprise me. For a man, he's not unintelligent."

From her that was high praise. Myrtale gave it an instant's pause. But the urgency that had awakened in her would not let her rest. "Tomorrow," she said, "whatever comes of it, I go hunting the witch from Thessaly."

"We'll hunt her together," said Timarete.

It was not as late as it might have been, nor had Philip drunk as deeply of the wine as he might have. He had been uneasy, crawling inside his skin, since shortly after his son was struck down. Some days were better than others, but tonight he was ready to damn the darkness, take a horse, and ride as far and fast as the beast could carry him.

Damned witches. He kicked open the door of his chamber, a petty thing but remarkably satisfying.

His Epirote wife sat beside the bed, wrapped in a mantle,

eyes glittering in the lamplight. It was a moment before he realized that as small and close as the room was, the air felt lighter here; cleaner. The nagging unease had faded almost to nothing.

She was doing it. It felt like warmth coming off her: not the heat of passion but a gentler thing, deeper and steadier.

Odd to think of anything gentle in connection with that one. Even now, her eyes on him were fierce, with intensity enough to set a man back on his heels.

She was not here to seduce him. The rush of heat at the sight of her gave way to almost painfully clear focus.

He had never looked at a woman before as he would a man or an equal. It was a strange sensation, made more so by the haze of wine. He pulled up a stool and perched on it and looked her straight in the face. "Tell me," he said.

She barely blinked. "I have to go away for a while. How long, I don't know, but I intend to be back before the baby comes. Long before, if the Mother has any care for me."

"What if I forbid you?" he asked—calmly, he thought; reasonably.

"That is not your place," she said.

He kept his temper in hand. He was proud of himself for it. "As long as you live in my palace and carry my son, it is most certainly my place."

Her face was blank. He wondered if she had heard him. "The air is full of lies and false memories. Those will only get worse. Try to remember the truth about me."

"You are not going," he said with force that should have rocked her where she sat.

Except for a slight widening of the eyes, she did not move at all. "I will come back," she said. "Living or dead. I promise you."

"I'll lock you up, then," he said, "and keep you there until my son is born."

"Our son," she said, "and even if you could hold me by any mortal means, that would only make it easier for our enemies to carry out their plan. They want us confined; they want us weak and frightened and subject to their will."

"Let them," he said. "I'll make war on their country. I'll kill their men and lay waste their fields and pastures. We'll see how eager they are then to raise up a puppet king in Macedon."

For an instant he thought she might concede that that was a sensible plan, but the moment of agreement passed; she shook her head. "You'll only scatter your resources and anger the witches, and make it worse for all."

"And you won't?"

"I will hunt them down," she said, "and rip out this sorcery by the roots." She spoke so softly he had to strain to hear her, and yet that softness was more convincing than any shout.

As she rose, he rose also. She drew his head down for a kiss. He stiffened, then all at once, whether through her witchery or because he had never been able to resist her, he surrendered.

There was the passion he had been missing, the fiery sweetness that he so well remembered. The pressure of her belly against his, the child rolling and kicking so strongly it must have bruised her, only made the kiss more potent.

He swam up from it, sucking in air. "Don't go," he said.

He was pleading now. She made no effort to argue; she simply brushed her fingers across his lips as if to silence him, or else to commit their shape to memory. "Be strong," she said. "Remember the truth of me."

He reached for her, but she was already out of reach.

She had left the lightness and the clarity behind her like a gift. Shadows hovered beyond it, visions of a world of grey-ness and confusion. In it, she was shut up in the women's quarters, and he had turned against her, and the source of his hatred was so strong and so clear that he almost could not stand against it: he came to her bed in the night, rigid with wanting her, and found her locked in passionate embrace with a huge and sickeningly supple snake.

He shook off that blatant absurdity and cast laughter in its face. "Is that the best you can do? I'll not fret for her, then."

He braced for a blast of fury, but the visions ran on blindly, growing dimmer as he turned his mind and heart away from them. He held in memory her face as he had last seen it, and her voice and her presence, the smell and taste of her, until they were all he saw and all he needed to see.

Twenty-five

It took most of Myrtale's strength to leave that room and that man and walk away without looking back. If he had called to her, she might have wavered, but it seemed he had surrendered at last to a woman's will—perhaps for the first time since he left his mother's breast.

Timarete waited in the shrine, all but invisible in the shadows. She was dressed for travel, even to the tall walking staff and the wanderer's pack.

For Myrtale she had the same, and no word wasted. Myrtale had been hoping for a magical transport or at the very least a mule to ride, but it seemed they were going to walk.

She had grown soft, sitting in palaces. She suppressed a sigh and let fall her soft rich chiton and her finely woven mantle to put on the rougher garb of a pilgrim. When she matched her aunt exactly, she took up the staff and shouldered the pack.

Timarete was already in motion. She was walking toward the door, but the way was unnaturally long and the texture of the darkness had changed.

Who needed ointments and false promises of flight when one could walk through the world rather than on it? Timarete waded through the substance of things as if it had been water. Myrtale, in her wake, felt the shifting tides of magic woven through with the warmth of the Mother's regard.

She was not hunting the enemy, not exactly, and yet she knew where Erynna was. The witch left a trail of scent in the aether, faint but distinct, like the stench of decay.

There were others with her, some so strong Myrtale gagged at them. Their trap was laid and the bait set; they waited with the patience of predators.

They would have Myrtale and the child she carried, no matter what she did or where she tried to do it. Despair was their weapon, and hopelessness, and fear. She should simply surrender and spare herself the trouble of fighting.

They were endlessly subtle and viciously inventive. Every thought she ventured to think, they were there before her. They had studied her thoroughly while she gathered such crumbs of magic as Erynna would share, the better to conquer her if she roused from the trance of misplaced trust and turned against them.

There was no use in either guilt or shame. Myrtale had done what she had done. Her child was still safe. Pella was as well protected as she or her aunt could manage.

They had passed beyond the palace and the city into featureless darkness. No stars or moon guided them; no road stretched before them. They floated in a sea of nothingness.

The dark was full of visions, surging and seething on the edge of sight. Flocks of shadows crowded in close; they chattered as the shades of the dead were said to do. Living women flew like birds above them, circling in the fitful light, singing an eerie song.

There was madness in that song. It stripped Myrtale of wits and sense, and bade fair to leave her as empty as the world into which she had fallen.

Timarete's hand gripped hers with bruising force. But stronger than that was the child within her, battering against the walls of the womb as if he would leap forth in full armor with spear in hand.

Pain was real. Pain was the world. It brought back the stars and set her feet on a hard and stony road.

Jagged peaks loomed above her. They had no names that she knew. The stars were all strange. The air was brutally cold, with a tang of iron.

Water roared below. A river ran through the gorge, cutting deep into the sheer walls. For a dizzy moment she thought it was a river of blood, so strong was the strangeness in the air, but such sanity as she had trickled back; she smelled the cold clarity of water.

The river's voice was manifold. Amid the roaring she heard shrieks and growls and what sounded like snatches of words, as if bodies tumbled in the torrent.

She could see nothing but mountains and stars, but her aunt's grip was strong still, her hand warm and blessedly alive. That warmth brought a memory of sunlight into this black and deadly place.

Myrtale realized she was crouching as if against a rain of blows. She straightened slowly. Her body ached; the child had quieted, although he was restless still.

He was not afraid, but his unease thrummed in her. She pressed her hands to the curve of her belly, willing reassurance into him. Those who had laid this trap wanted him alive; they would not harm him while he lay in the womb.

That was true, but she walled off the rest of the thought: that Myrtale needed only to be warm and breathing in order to bring him to birthing. What the witches had done to Arrhidaios, they could do to her. Witless, senseless, and pliable, she would be no more than a vessel for their puppet king.

The horror of that all but overwhelmed her. Almost too late, she recoiled from this latest of many subtle spells.

Dear Mother, they knew her too well; she was too weak, too young, too ill-schooled. She should never have come here, never have challenged them. She should have stayed in Pella.

"Stop." Timarete's voice cracked like a whip. Slow light dawned in the chasm, laying bare the stark cliffs and the turbulence of the river.

They stood on a shelf of rock midway down the crag. Behind them was darkness absolute—but it breathed. Myrtale shuddered with sudden cold.

Wherever they had been, Timarete's lone word had brought them to living earth and familiar sky. A cavern opened in the crag. With no evidence of either fear or hesitation, Timarete stepped into the darkness.

Myrtale dug in her heels, but her aunt's grip was relentless. Stone remained solid underfoot; in the dark she heard the river's roar fading with unnatural rapidity, until she stumbled forward in whispering quiet.

The walls closed in: the air grew thicker and the floor rougher. Timarete's pace slowed, which was merciful: more than once, Myrtale lost her footing and nearly fell.

The way, which had been level, began gradually to ascend.

Her breath came harder; her sight, if she had had any, would have begun to dim.

This was eerily like the ascent of the Mysteries on Samothrace, but there was a profound difference in it. That had been blessed in all its parts. This was anything but blessed, and deadly dangerous.

When Myrtale could not have borne the burden of her body for another step, sudden light dazzled her. It was the barest glimmer ahead, but as her aunt drew her onward, it brightened to the pallor of moonlight, although there was no moon tonight.

The sound of water rose again, but softer, less a roar now than a whisper. With it came the scent of greenery, the sharpness of bay and thyme. Cool night air wafted over her.

The light revealed itself to be a lamp encased in pale stone. A handful of tall pale men rose from where they had been sitting. Myrtale remembered none of their names but one, but their family she did indeed remember: the Hymenides, those last remnants of the old people from the vale of Acheron.

Young Attalos would not look directly at her, though she caught the flash of his glance. His brothers were equally shy, or maybe that was veiled contempt. They bowed low to Timarete.

"Enough of that," the priestess said. "Time's wasting. Is it all done as I bade?"

"All of it, lady," said the eldest.

"Good, then," she said. "Let's begin."

The Hymenides fell in like an honor guard, surrounding the two women. Their lamp lit the way along the narrow bank of the river, beneath cliffs fully as steep as those on the other side of the cavern. This river was gentler by a little, and narrower and shallower, but it was still a great power in this world or any other.

Myrtale was beyond exhaustion. She walked because if she did not, they would carry her; and that would be more humiliation than she could bear. She had stopped wondering how, in this state, she could do battle with anything but her own body.

One thing alone she was sure of. The witches were waiting. The river's flood led to them; so did the wheeling of the stars, and the voices of the dead chittering about her. This was the living world, but the dark land was as close as her chiton to her skin. To touch it, she had only to reach out her hand.

The dead needed blood, Erynna had told her—as had her teachers before that, and old Homer himself in his tales of her ancestors. Maybe that was true, but living blood in living body was at least as strong a lure as blood of sacrifice poured out upon the earth.

Myrtale's strength was coming back. The earth fed it; the stars called it forth. Even her guards offered what they had, whether they knew it or no.

Her steps steadied. When the track ascended, she barely quailed. The stars were fading; she could see the shadow of a wall above her.

They were in Acheron indeed, and the place to which they had come was the great shrine, the Nekromanteion, high above the river. Mountains marched away below it, sheer slopes and sudden crags as far as she could see.

There should have been priests here, attendants, pilgrims dreaming in the hidden rooms and descending into the caverns where the visions were. But there was no living soul in all that place but Myrtale and her companions. Tonight it was theirs, their battlefield, poised between the mortal world and the world of magic.

The dead were there in plenty. They flocked like sparrows, crowding thick over the altar and trailing like mist above the walls. The murmur of their voices drowned out the river; the wind they raised overcame the wind of earth.

Were they the witches' weapon, then? Would they drain the life out of her, leaving only enough to bring the child forth alive?

"They're not the trap," Timarete said, standing side by side with her in mind as in body. "They're simply a diversion."

Myrtale shuddered. However diligently the priestesses in Dodona had labored to teach her not to fear the shades of the dead, the thought of them was a cold chill down her spine.

She stiffened her back and restrained herself from creeping under Timarete's mantle. For this night above all, she needed courage.

The altar lay before her. In place of the blood sacrifices of these late days, it was heaped with offerings of an older time: flowers of the early spring, fruits far out of season, garlands of myrtle and bay. Without stopping to think, she lifted one of myrtle and crowned herself with it.

Its pungent scent surrounded her. The hordes of the dead swirled like smoke. They brought a memory: Philip's strong warm hands cupping her face, and the taste of his lips on hers.

That brought her to herself. The earth was deep and strong beneath her. She knelt, the better to feel that strength, and laid her hands on the stony ground. Soft new grass sprang through her fingers.

It was growing as she knelt there, both blessing and promise. The child stirred in response. His heart was the core of the sun. Darkness had no power against him.

It was all around them, more powerful than the dead. The enemy had come behind the wall of it, driving it before them.

Twenty-six

Myrtale saw through the darkness with ease that should not have been possible. The light inside her cast itself through the walls of the world, and the earth's power rose up through her. She saw the forces that had hunted her all her life, and committed their faces to memory.

Erynna was one of them, not quite the least but far from the greatest. Those rode a black wind, flying as Myrtale had seen in her dream or vision: a phalanx of witches clothed in naught but the ointment that bore the magic.

They drifted like leaves above the shrine. The flocks of the dead had fled in terror. Myrtale knew no fear of them, even as she recognized the power that beat down upon her.

The Hymenides buckled under it. Their weapons were useless, their magic too frail to withstand the onslaught. Their bodies were a shield still, to death if need be; in that, even now, they never wavered.

Only Timarete stood upright. If she felt herself outnumbered, she did not show it. Light kindled in the staff she had brought from Pella.

Pride might have brought Myrtale to her feet, but she

needed the earth's strength more than she needed such bravado. She sat on her heels, hands still flat in the thickening grass.

She braced for thunderbolts and the casting of mighty spells. What came was much more dangerous.

The woman who alighted amid the offerings on the altar was neither young nor old, neither beautiful nor ugly. Her hair was no particular color in the dimming starlight; her skin was pale, her body more thin than plump. She was as ordinary as a person could be, and that in itself was powerful magic.

She had a rod in her hand, a peeled wand. She carried it casually, held lightly in her fingers, as if it had no significance. And yet at the sight of it, Myrtale doubled up with sudden, piercing pain.

Her mind babbled to itself. They wanted her child. They needed him—alive and enslaved to their will. They would not harm him now, nor force him into the world before he could survive there.

This was a feint. It had to be. It could not—

Myrtale thrust panic aside. It was part of the spell, meant to weaken her until all thought of attack or defense was driven from her mind. Then they would have her, and the child, beyond hope of escape.

One of the Hymenides rose up with startling speed and hurled his spear direct to the witch's heart.

It passed through her as if through a swirl of mist. Even as she laughed at him, her rod flicked out to brush his cheek.

He withered like a leaf in a flame. Before his brothers could utter a word, he had crumbled to dust. A gust of wind scattered it, dissolving it into nothingness.

Attalos howled and lunged. Timarete's outthrust arm flung him back before he could go the way of his elder brother. The rest, having more sense or less crazy courage, hung well back but kept their spears balanced in their hands.

In a movement so smooth it seemed slow, but in truth it was preternaturally fast, Timarete flung her own spear, a spear of magic. That, unlike the mortal weapon, struck its target; but the witch twisted, eluding the worst of it. It rocked but did not destroy her.

While she swayed, Timarete struck again and yet again. On the fourth stroke, the witches who had hovered, watching, gathered in a flock high above her.

They looked like hawks poised for the kill. Myrtale, for the moment forgotten, gathered as much strength as she could. Knowledge, she had too little of, but she had never needed it to bring down the sun.

This was her own earth, her country, her Epiros, that embraced this vale of Acheron. Had they forgotten that, and remembered only that here in the black vale, where death and darkness ruled, their magic was all the stronger?

They were not such fools as that. They had come in force, they had chosen the place of battle, and now they surrounded her, barring every path of escape.

The child had gone still inside her. She might have thought little of that, had she not come to see how subtle the witches truly were. Serpent subtlety: creeping in shadows, striking the heel.

Nearly invisible tendrils of magic had unfolded from the witch's rod. Even as the witch defended herself against Timarete's relentless attack, the rod went on weaving its spell.

It was almost beautiful, that work of the darkest art. It bound a soul as tightly as a spider bound its prey, numbed his spirit and suborned his will but left him free to walk and talk and live as a mortal man. He would be king in Macedon, and he would fulfill the destiny that had been woven for him—but how and when and for whom he did it would be entirely in their hands.

They would make him great, for their own purposes. He would rule as they bade him, nor would he know to care.

Deep in Myrtale's heart, she tasted bitter laughter. Her aunt had done nearly the same to her, albeit with the best of intentions. Now they both paid, Timarete no less than Myrtale.

Myrtale's son would not pay. As foolish as it might be, she raised her head and looked Erynna in the face.

Erynna smiled. The air around her filled with certainties. Yes, let Myrtale win this battle. Let her son be born and live uncorrupted. Then let her know the true depth of her folly, when he abandoned her to conquer the world. He would look on her with love and loathing; he would go the way he chose, without regard to any other, least of all the woman who had borne him.

"There is no gratitude in that heart," Erynna said. Her voice spoke in Myrtale's ear, as if she stood close by and not far above her. "He will defy you in every way, thwart you, oppose you, mock you and all your purposes. Then he will die long before his time, leaving you amid the ruins of his empire."

"Maybe," said Myrtale, "but he'll do it of his own will. He'll be no crushed and trammeled thing."

"That's a pretty dream," said Erynna, "until you wake and see how grim a life you've bound yourself to. We've seen all the twists that fate can weave into the tapestry. You will curse the day you refused us, and mourn the death of all your dreams."

A gust of fetid wind buffeted Myrtale. This was more than a curse; it was truth, spoken with the voice of power. For all her resolve, Myrtale wavered.

Would it be so terrible after all if her child were guided rather than left free to choose his own destiny?

"Yes," Erynna breathed in her ear. "Come with us; help us shape the world. With such magic as you have, the world can be yours, and everything in it. Your son can be anything you wish him to be."

Around them, the battle had subsided into stillness. The witch on the altar was battered and bleeding but still upright. Timarete balanced a spear of lightning in her hand with improbable ease, but did not cast it.

They were all, witches and priestess alike, watching Myrtale. It was all in her hands.

Hers, not Erynna's. The child rode within her body. The divinity that had made him, the magic that filled him, came through her. Until he was born, no one but Myrtale could make his choices for him.

A great anger swelled up in her, an eruption of rage that either of them should be forced to this. Did they think her so weak that she was fair prey for every snake that lurked in the grass, and every hawk that flew overhead?

And yet as she reached for the sun that lived in the heart of her, her eye caught Erynna's. The witch was smiling. Even this was a trap. It was all a trap, every moment of it.

Or was that the trap—to freeze her into immobility, incapable of choosing a course, until they overwhelmed her mind and cast her down?

She thrust the thought aside. Whether she acted well or ill, she must act. She must choose.

There was no sun to draw down. It was still below the horizon. She drew it up out of the earth into the waiting sky.

It strained in her grasp, struggling to escape. The stab of

fear came near to destroying her. But she was not the child who had toppled a mountain. She had a little sense now, and a scrap or two of discipline.

It could not be enough. No mortal should meddle with such powers as these. Flesh and bone were not strong enough to hold them.

She must not give way to doubt. The sun grew within her, even as it swelled through earth into sky. The witches shrieked and thrashed. Bolts of magic blistered the air around her.

None of them touched her. The sun seared them to nothing, blazing as bright as a summer noon. It swept them out of the sky.

That great winnowing left Myrtale at the eye of creation, laid bare to every eye that could see magic.

Some of the witches had fallen, but too many rose again, swirling together, linked hand in hand. As they spun above her, her eye caught on the wheel and fixed. Both thought and sense fled away.

Pain shot through her, flinging her backward. The child dealt one last, agonizing blow, then subsided into deceptive quiet.

For a precious moment, her mind was her own again. The sun had all but escaped her grasp. She lunged, her whole spirit a prayer, and caught it. With more hope than art or skill, she smote the wheel of witches even as their cloud of hopelessness enveloped her.

The sun died. She gave herself up to the final blow— knowing that while her body might live, her mind would be gone. She would be as witless as her son's elder brother, his only living rival for the throne on which the witches would set him.

The ember of anger within her flared—feeble after the soaring fire of the sun, but it warmed her just enough. By its light she saw the stony hillside in the grey light of dawn, and the shrine of the dead standing stark on its summit, and of the witches nothing, not even a rag or a bone.

They had all burned away in that last eruption of light. She was alone in the shrine—utterly alone, until a sound brought her about.

Timarete swayed on her feet. Her face was blank, as if both thought and emotion had been seared away. There was still magic in her, but it burned perilously low.

Myrtale had not known she had any left herself, until it stroked her aunt with healing and with peace. Timarete sighed and sank to her knees.

She was still conscious. Her eyes when they lifted to Myrtale were clear. There was no more awe in them than ever, but perhaps there was a glimmer of respect. She inclined her head. "You've done well," she said.

Myrtale was not looking for praise. She rose stiffly. The child was so still that her hands flew to her center in a flare of pure terror—but he was alive. He was exhausted, as were they all, but he was well; he would live.

She could not collapse in relief. She was a long way from Pella. However she managed to return there, return she must. She had a husband waiting, and friends and kin, and a son to bring into the world.

He would be born free, and the world would be his to rule. No one and nothing would bind him, except honor and glory and—she could hope—love for his kin, and most particularly his mother.

Epilogue

After so bitter a winter, spring that year was unusually beautiful. The air was soft, the rain fell lightly; the fields were full of flowers.

In Pella, every child who was born in that season both lived and thrived. Even poor witless Arrhidaios seemed to find a fragment of his former self. He learned to laugh again, and to walk, and even, as summer drew near, to fall into a stumbling run.

Summer was no gentler than it ever was in these mountains, but it brought victory for the king both in battle and in the games at Olympia. Philip was a happy man, and he brought that happiness into the portico where Myrtale spent her days, sitting by her as often as not and entertaining her with stories.

The witches' curse had died with them. The curse in men's minds was less inclined to wither away; rumors flew still, lies and distortions that would have plagued Myrtale if she had been in any frame of mind to care. Even the sight of her king looking after her with tender solicitude fed their malice. He was ensorcelled, they said; she had enslaved him to her will.

The time would come when she dealt with that. It barely

dimmed these long bright days, this golden time of waiting for her son to be born. The heavier and more unwieldy she grew, the less she cared for anything but the child within her and his father beside her.

Timarete had gone back to Dodona after she rode the tide of their mingled magic to Pella, but at midsummer she appeared again, this time with an embassy from the king of Epiros. Arybbas had sent gifts to his niece and her royal husband, and tribute to the child who was to be born.

Myrtale was happier to see her aunt than she might have expected. Timarete was no different in words or actions; the battle at the shrine of the dead might never have happened at all— except for one thing.

Myrtale had some understanding now of what she was and why she did as she did. It was enough, just, to ease the tension between them, though Myrtale had not forgiven Timarete for a lifetime of ignorance. That might never come to pass, but it was no longer so strong as to poison every word they spoke to one another.

They could almost be friends. Myrtale would never in this world have expected that.

They had more in common than either of them liked to admit, Myrtale reflected one breathlessly hot morning. She had lain abed well past sunrise: it was difficult, these days, to shift her bulk. Nevertheless she did at length make her way to the portico in search of such relief from the heat as there might be.

There was a faint breeze wafting up from the lake, just enough to taunt her with promises. She lay on the couch that Philip had given her, that had come all the way from Persia. Its arms were carved in the shapes of fantastical beasts; she smoothed the curves of one elaborately arched neck and reflected on the ways in which even the most obstinate mortal creature could change.

Timarete was never so feeble as to succumb to heat. She looked as cool as she ever had, sitting upright on the bench that Philip tended to favor.

He was not there this morning, but Myrtale had no reason to fret. This time of day, he held court in the hall, hearing disputes and giving judgment. She could have gone to listen, if she had had any will to move.

The weight of air was heavy on her, even heavier than the heat. Only the Mother's snake and her own hatchling seemed in comfort. They basked in sunlight, stretched long and glistening across the pavement.

As her eyes rested on them, the hatchling stirred, slithering toward her couch. It was quite large now, almost as large as the Mother's snake—and that was no small creature. When it raised its head and half of its body, its unblinking eyes were level with the edge of the couch. It poured itself up over what was left of her lap, coiling against her side. She closed her eyes and sighed.

She lacked the will to move or speak, nor did Timarete break the silence. Each of them had said everything that could or should be said. Now they only had to wait and watch and hope, until the child was born.

What would happen then, how he would grow, what kind of man he could be—that was his to choose. Myrtale had refused to do it for him. He was free as every man is, to live the life the Mother had given him.

Her body was never in comfort these days, but she had expected that; she had learned to endure the aches, the heaviness, even the occasional sharp pain. This was a new kind of pain, and yet she recognized it from a deep well of memory.

She was not afraid. She never was, not of the great things. She spoke without opening her eyes. "It's time," she said.

All the long slow months of waiting gathered into this moment. The languor of the summer morning erupted into a flurry, with her aunt marshaling troops as briskly as any general.

Myrtale's mind was at once clouded and clear. Her body seemed distant and rather alien, as if it belonged to someone else. She knew, equally distantly, that the alternation of all-encompassing pain and all too brief respite might seem to last as long as the rest of these nine months.

She had time enough and more to search out the roots of magic, to sink deep into the earth and to touch the sky. Dread had lingered in her that even yet there might be an assault against her or her son, but that truly was done. The only danger now would be his own self, his strong will and his proud spirit.

That would be a fair fight. It began here in the chamber to which Timarete saw her carried, where the midwives waited—an army of them, so many that Timarete dismissed them summarily, leaving only the most skilled. That one and a handful of deft and quiet servants waited out the hours, giving her what comfort they could.

He was eager to leap into the world—too eager. The pain blurred into a single long moment of agony. Voices babbled, feet ran swiftly, now swelling close, now fading away.

She could die. As long as he lived, she hardly cared. She would rule among the dead, then, where the Mother was still strong, and the world was not all given to the whims of men.

Odd that she should come round to that now, in the most female of all rites, for which every woman was made. Her son, her strong male child, tried to rip his way out of her. If he had had a sword, he would have cloven her in two.

She would not let that be an omen. She had magic still; she had the earth and the sky. They were all around her always.

She enfolded him in them. She soothed his vaunting eagerness; she taught him, not to be gentle, but to stop and think and consider how best to conquer—not always by force; sometimes by subtlety, too.

Twice she had brought down the sun. Now she brought its child into the world, a fiery spirit and a presence so strong it would yield to no mortal power.

It yielded to her. A great cry burst out of her, a cry more of triumph than of pain.

For all the weight of fear and hope and foresight that they had laid on him, he was as unprepossessing an object as any other newborn child. Myrtale looked down into the small, crumpled, crimson face and knew both cold clarity and a love so fierce, so strong, so all-consuming that it left her gasping.

She knew exactly what he was and would be. A man—with all the good and the ill that went with it. A king—of that she had no more doubt now than she had since he was conceived. An adversary, maybe, as he grew in his own way and with his own will.

Philip's shadow fell across her. He recoiled even as he bent to peer at his son, startled by the snake that nestled between the child and his mother. Then he caught himself; his breath hissed, but he bent again, lifted the swaddled bundle from her arms and held it up.

"His name is Alexander," Myrtale said.

She braced for resistance—after all, he would be expecting to name the child himself—but although he paused to consider the name, no frown darkened his brow. He nodded. "Alexander," he said.

He should go, take their child away and acknowledge him before the people, but he lingered. He had never been eager to leave her—nor, if she had her way, would he ever be.

He bent and set a kiss on her forehead. "You," he said, "deserve a new name yourself. Lady of power, lady of victories, I name you Olympias: for you ran your own great race, and brought home the crown."

She took time to consider that, as he had considered the name she gave his son. It was not a long moment, though maybe long enough for his patience. In it she felt her old name falling away, casting off her former self as a snake would shed its skin.

"Yes," she said at last. "Yes, I am that, both lady and queen. I am Olympias."